SAM HANNA BELL was born in Glasgow in 1909 of Ulster
emigrant parents. On the death of his father, a journalist, he
was brought 'home' to Ireland at the age of seven to be reared
in the Strangford Lough area of County Down, where his
acclaimed novel of Ulster rural life, *December Bride* (1951), is
set. He worked during the 1950s, 1960s and 1970s as a senior
features producer with the BBC Northern Ireland Region,
pioneering the collection and broadcasting of fast-vanishing
folklore and folk music from remote country areas. He
continued to write during this period and after retirement; his
other novels are *The Hollow Ball* (1961), *A Man Flourishing*
(1973) and *Across the Narrow Sea* (1987). In 1970 Queen's
University Belfast awarded him the honorary degree of MA for
achievements in the arts. He died in February 1990.

FROM A PENCIL DRAWING BY DORIS V. BLAIR

ERIN'S ORANGE LILY

AND

SUMMER LOANEN
and other stories

•

SAM HANNA BELL

THE
BLACKSTAFF
PRESS

BELFAST

FRONTISPIECE

Facsimile of first edition frontispiece,
Summer Loanen and Other Stories

Erin's Orange Lily first published in 1956 by
Dobson Books Limited, London W8
and printed by
The Garden City Press Limited, Letchworth, Herts

Summer Loanen and Other Stories first published in 1943 by
The Mourne Press, Newcastle, County Down, Northern Ireland
and printed by
The Banbridge Chronicle Press, Banbridge, County Down

This edition of *Erin's Orange Lily* and *Summer Loanen and Other Stories*
(as one volume) is a photolithographic facsimile of the 1956 Dobson Books edition
and the 1943 Mourne Press edition published in 1996 by
The Blackstaff Press Limited
3 Galway Park, Dundonald, Belfast BT16 0AN, Northern Ireland

Printed in Ireland by ColourBooks Limited

A CIP catalogue record for this book
is available from the British Library

ISBN 0-85640-589-2

SAM HANNA BELL

ERIN'S ORANGE LILY

LONDON: DENNIS DOBSON

For
my son
FERGUS

I do herein rely upon those bards or Irish chronicles . . . unto them besides I add mine own reading; and out of them both together, with comparison of times, likewise of manners and customs, affinity of words and names, properties of nature and uses, resemblances of rites and ceremonies, and many other like circumstances, I do gather a likelihood of truth, not certainly affirming anything, but by conferring of times, language, monuments and such like, I do hunt out a probability of things, which I leave to your judgment to believe or refuse.

(Edmund Spenser, *View of the State of Ireland*, 1595.)

CONTENTS

The decoration at the head of Chapter I is by William Conor, R.H.A., and is reproduced by permission of the artist; Chapter II is from *Wild Sports of the West* by W. H. Maxwell (1832); Chapter III an engraving of Long Bridge, Belfast, after George Petrie, R.H.A. (1829); Chapter IV from *The Whiskey Distilleries of the United Kingdom* by Alfred Barnard (1887); Chapter VI from *The Irish Sketchbook* by W. M. Thackeray (1842); Chapters V and IX from *Sketches of Irish Character* by Mrs. S. C. Hall; Chapters VII and VIII from *Ireland, Its Scenery and Character* by Mr. and Mrs. S. C. Hall.

FOREWORD

Into the nine chapters of this book I have gathered a few of the traditions and customs of the Nine Counties of historic Ulster. Here and there the story runs beyond the confines of the northern Province, for a custom is no more susceptible to borders than is the social activity from which it arises; whether it is a way of preaching or of ploughing, a fashion in knitting socks or of netting salmon.

The numerical coincidence of chapters and counties is fortuitous. I have not surveyed the social lore of each county and there are ninety-nine, if not a hundred, Ulster customs which the reader, with justification, might expect to find in a book such as this. But the selection is not as arbitrary as may at first appear for I have included only those customs of which I have some knowledge, or at some time have enjoyed with my neighbours.

This book, then, is not the work of a folklorist; and I feel no more put out by this admission than if I had to confess that I am not a potter or a prophet or a private eye. But the genuine folklorist (I have met one or two) is all three rolled into one; he has to have the patience of Job, the persistence of Palissy, the deductive powers of Sherlock Holmes, and if you have a pet definition of a sceptic you can throw that in too. Add to this a knowledge of shards and shreds, music and monoliths, an ability to converse with fellow-savants in a dozen languages and dialects, and you have the profile of a folklorist. All that I bring to these pages is a lively curiosity in what my fellow-citizens do and how they do it, and the good fortune that in my daily work as a B.B.C. Features producer this curiosity is encouraged.

Since this book was written an Ulster Folklore Committee has been organised. This new organisation will have no lack of work lying to its hand, and, I am certain, no lack of men and women eager to assist in that work. Most certainly it is not before its time, for the old ways of our community are vanishing rapidly. A visitor to Ireland wishing to enrich the cathedral of his native city asked a bishop where he might secure relics of an Irish saint. The bishop replied: 'Go into any graveyard, the most remote in the land, and take a handful of dust. So you will have your relics.' In another generation the same answer will hold for those who search Ulster for the relics of men lesser than saints.

Chapter One

TO CHAP THE LAMBEG

A<small>N ULSTERMAN WAS WATCHING</small> a procession in Manchester. As one of the brass bands of which the North of England is so justifiably proud passed, a Mancunian said: 'There's a *real* band for you. Pity you didn't have one or two like that in Ireland.' 'Aye,' agreed the Ulsterman readily. 'They'd get the chance of walking in a *real* procession.'

He could have reminded his friend that once upon a time St Joseph's Brass and Reed Band from Newry in County Down lifted the Bellevue Championship from the English bands and brought it to Ireland. Of that memorable occasion perhaps he knew nothing. As an Ulsterman he was more than a competent judge of processions.

Fortunately for us history has dictated that our great processions should celebrate in the summer months. The

Loyal Orange Lodges walk on the 12th of July, the Ancient
Order of Hibernians on the 15th of August, and the Royal
Black Preceptory on the last Saturday of August. Of these
the Orange Procession, being the largest, is the most
important, for no matter how estimable are the aims of a
fraternity a procession remains pageantry, and pageantry
without spectators is an idleness. We have a Bank Holiday,
therefore, on the 12th of July.

The Orangemen have their dramatic traditions and when
I speak of traditions I don't mean fictions, for many of them
have been contributed by the tumultuous history of Ireland.
They are painted on their banners: The Closing of the
Gates of Derry by the Apprentice Boys; The Death of
Schomberg; the *Mountjoy* Breaking the Boom that barred
the Foyle (perhaps the most striking banner of the lot, for
no matter how sedately the bearers walk, every tremor and
pulsation across the silk gives vivacity to the swelling sails,
the billowing clouds and the curling smoke from the
Mountjoy's cannon); and the final scene when King
William, copied with variations from the original painting
by Sir Benjamin West, faces his royal opponent across the
Boyne Water.

The Bible is prominent on Orange banners. The Open
Bible rests on its cushion; Queen Victoria exemplifies
the Secret of England's Greatness by handing a Bible
to a suppliant Negro. 'No matter who's carrying that
banner now,' a banner-painter told me, 'it was first
ordered by Episcopalians. It was always a great favourite
among that persuasion.' The Dove returns to the Ark;

Elijah is fed by the ravens, and David goes up against
Goliath:

From the brook five stones he took, and placed them in his scrip;
Undauntedly across the plain this gallant youth did trip;
At his first blow he laid him low, cut off his head forbye,
He dropped his sling and they made a king of this young Shepherd's
   Boy.

       .   .   .   .   .

So fill the glass, round let it pass for I am getting dry,
And toast with me the memory of this young Shepherd's Boy.

Which reminds us that the Orangemen could allegorise
their King-Hero as aptly as the Jacobites.

   Nature also conspires to assist at Orange pageantry. In
July the countryman's garden is garrisoned with Sweet
William and the Orange Lily, for it is said that King William
on his way to the Boyne plucked a spray of Orange Lily
and bore it as his emblem.

Let dandies fine, in Bond Street shine, gay nymphs in Piccadilly, O!
But fine or gay must yield the day, to Erin's Orange Lily, O!
Then come brave boys, and share her joys, and toast the health of
   Willy, O!
Who bravely wore, on Boyne's red shore, the Royal Orange
   Lily, O!

   There are other traditions as yet lacking documentary
proof. King William when he landed in Ireland left the
imprint of his foot on the quay at Carrickfergus, and the
man who signed the first Orange warrant, lacking a quill
and ink, drew blood from his hand with a thorn and signed
with a sprig of hyssop. "Tis best that way,' says he, 'for

the first Orange warrant should not be written by anything made by the hand of man!'

If these stories have never been proved I hope they will never be disproved, for the Protestant Ulsterman is not too richly hanselled in tales of wonder.

★

Much of the pugnacity has gone from the music played on the 12th of July. Nowadays the bands rarely strike up the lively party airs like *Dolly's Brae*, *Slitter-Slatter*, or *Up Comes a Man*. A stranger reading the lyrics usually attached to these melodies by some 'Collector and Arranger' would think them colourless enough; and he would be right. But these chunks of poesy bear no resemblance whatever to the words evoked in most Ulstermen when they hear the tunes played. The sentiment of John de Jean Fraser that

> *The same good soil sustaining both*
> *Makes both united flourish*
> *But cannot give the Orange growth*
> *And cease the Green to nourish*

would have received scant sympathy from the bards long since dead and forgotten whose ballads I learnt in my childhood. Neither they nor their verse suffered from ambiguous doctrine or enervating liberalism. The genial tale of the *Ould Orange Flute* is now a comic ditty sung with as much gusto by the Roman Catholic as the Protestant. Obviously if such a tendency were to continue it could result only in frustration for everybody. The original Orange ballad-makers insured against any possibility of that.

To the Ulsterman a flute band blows the music closest to his heart and most familiar to his ears. I suppose all the members of flute bands are accomplished musicians nowadays, but I remember the time when the country band often employed a 'dummy flute' to achieve symmetry in the ranks of its flautists. The flute wasn't given to just anybody of course, for to blow convincingly, finger and apparently rid the instrument of spittle with a flick of the wrist demanded an apt sense of mimicry.

To-day the Twelfth bands content themselves with march tunes, hymns and innocuous Irish airs. But every now and again the melodious procession is punctuated by the tyrannical thunder of the Lambeg drums. They usually travel in pairs, beaten or *chapped* by shirt-sleeved men, and as they trot past, for the drummers have to take two paces to the bandsman's one, their reverberations drown every other sound, set windows chattering in their frames and print a stunned smile on the face of the onlooker. 'They're like two men quarrelling at a funeral,' an Englishman once said to me. But (apart from his inept comparison to the *locus citatus*) that is precisely what they are *not* doing

The Lambeg drums are beaten to the rhythm of a hornpipe, reel or jig. If you're inclined to doubt this you might try bawling a hornpipe at the top of your voice the next time you hear them. I can recommend *The Ha'penny Gate*, or better still, *Willie John's Breakdown*. At one time the drummers were always led and controlled by a fifer. Even if the onlookers never heard him the drummers picked up enough of the shrill notes to help keep them in time. If necessary the fifer danced round and round in front of the drums or walked backwards on the line of march.

Except in some country districts the fifer has dropped out of fashion and in most places, Belfast particularly, the aspirants pick up their rhythm and tempo from gramophone records. The Englishman was mistaken in thinking that the two drummers were trying to shout each other down. Their intention, whether they achieved it or not, was unison. If they have no fifer with them the old hand curbs his virtuosity in rolls and double-chaps to suit his less experienced partner. As one old drummer said, 'they're like two dancers dancing, only instead of using their feet they're dancing their canes on the drumheads. If they're doing it properly the two drums'll sound like one.'

The drumming-match is another matter. Here it is not unison between the drummers but rivalry. Each is endeavouring to throw the other into confusion with missed chaps, faster and more intricate rolling, or just an overwhelming volume of sound. Nor is this all, for it is at the same time a contest between the drums. If I have a drum made by say Mahaffy, and a likely man has a drum made by McIlveen, convention permits me to challenge him in one of two traditional forms: either, 'Are you game for a stick-in?' or less curtly, 'Would you like a bit of a tune?' But if we discover that our drums were made by the same craftsman my challenge is unacceptable and I have to go on seeking until I find a drummer whose drum was built by hands other than those of Mr Mahaffy.

The contestants take up their stand facing each other and

the stick-in is on. And here I must confess the *mystique* of the contest eludes me, for while due consideration is given to dexterity, consistence in tempo and powerful chapping, at the same time the 'tone and ring' of the drum is of great importance. Would it be possible for a poor drummer with a good drum to defeat a good drummer with a poor drum? I've never had a satisfactory answer to that, but I think it probable that the good drummer would get the verdict— if there was one. For while there is generally a ring of experts around the contestants they discreetly keep their opinions to themselves. There was a traditional way of giving a verdict and that was when an onlooker snatched off his cap, rushed into the ring and planted it on top of what, in his opinion, was the victor's drum. But as my informant added with a grim smile, 'he probably wouldn't be needing it for a day or two', it seemed to imply a certain excess of enthusiasm.

The 'tone and ring' of a Lambeg drum is the result of a number of calculated and nicely balanced factors. The oak shell has, of course, to be of expert workmanship, but the tightening of the drum-heads or skins is of vital importance. I can do no better than repeat a description of this operation told me by a fervid Lambegger.

'The head is only paper thickness so you have to be very careful when you're tightening them. Say you took on a drumming match for next Saturday—well, on Monday night you would put the heads on your drum and lace her up. You would tighten her a wee bit and chap her a wee bit. Then the next night you would tighten her a wee bit more and chap a bit, and so on till you have her like a bell on

the Saturday. You couldn't sleep in your bed when the
drums for a match are in the house. They're cracking all
night—giving all the time. Do you know this? If you were
to set a half-bucket of water under a drum by accident
she would drink it up in a night. I've seen us going down
from Belfast to Carrickfergus for a match with our
drums as hard as boards, and by the time we got near the
shore you might as well have been beating a wet dishclout.'

To a Lambegger his drum is always a 'bell' and 'tone and
ring' is the quality most sought after. The association can be
traced in the names of such famous drums as *The Bell of
Ballylisnahuncheon* and *The Chiming Bells of Laurel Vale*.
But one man's imagery makes an iconoclast of the next;
a drum-maker told me that he once had an order from a
man who had decided to name his drum *Roarin' Meg*
after the famous cannon employed at the defence of
Derry. Unfortunately the man died before he could take
delivery.

The custom of naming Lambeg drums is an old one and
the names are usually associated with a Lodge or district,
such as *The Tullyhue Queen* which bears a portrait of Queen
Victoria. But there are also Lambeggers who, although
they drum at the head of a Lodge on the 12th of July or the
15th of August, are not necessarily members of the Orange
Order or of the Hibernians. They may be members of a
Drumming Club or solitary voices shouting across two
or three townlands. The drums which may have been in
their families for over half-a-century often bear, as a
memorial, the portrait of the owner's father or grandfather;
a sort of speaking likeness.

The Orangeman's explanation of the custom of Hunting the Wren is explained in the following tag:

> *The Wren and the Robin*
> *leapt upon the drum*
> *and wakened up the Orangemen*
> *before the Ribbonmen come.*

There are several such rhymes and stories linking the origin of the Lambeg drum with the fateful intervention of birds. The most popular of these relates an incident at the Battle of the Boyne when the Dutch Guards after a forced march from Dundalk were allowed to break ranks so that they might eat some of their ration. One little drummer-boy was so exhausted that when he had eaten his food on the head of his drum he nodded over asleep. A bird settled on the drum and its pecking on the skin roused the boy. He opened his eyes to see the Duke of Berwick's Horse entering the river in an attempt to outflank his comrades. He jumped to his feet, beat an alarm, and the Jacobite cavalry were turned. The incident was later recalled and the chapping of the Lambeg represents the pecking beak of the bird—presumably of a species now extinct. It is a pretty story but rather doubtful history.

The intervention of the bird has a biblical flavour which appeals to the Orangeman; it testifies that Providence is on his side. But there is a more plausible if prosaic explanation for the Lambeg. In the Broomhedge district of County Antrim within living memory the Lambeg was accompanied by a snare-drum and fife, in another district it is accompanied only by the fife, and in a third (indeed in most districts) the fife has been discarded and the drum appears as a solo instrument. It seems reasonable to me to deduce from this that the big bass drum of a country band was the archetype, the original of the Lambeg, and that the men of Broomhedge were the last to play it in the traditional way accompanied by the remnants of a band in the shape of a snare-drum and fife.

If this is accepted as at least being plausible the rest of the story follows smoothly enough. There is, in the City of Belfast, a well-known firm of drum-makers; in the year 1870 the great-grandfather of the present generation, that is the founder of the firm, made the first shell drum. Until then bass drums had been built up with staves, rather like a barrel, but in 1870 came this new drum made from a single oak board curved to make the shell and joined at the over-lapping seam. That first shell drum, which is still in existence, was built for Moira Orange Lodge No. 39 and was played in 1871 at the Orange Demonstration in Lambeg from which district these drums take their name.

The drummers of Broomhedge had a further contri-bution to make to the art of Lambegging. In 1896 one Frank Carey discarded the buff-headed sticks and adopted the canes with which the drum is chapped at the present day. The idea presumably was to extract even more noise.

Drums are by their very nature noisy, but the sustained roar of the Lambegs is a sore point in many Ulster towns and villages. Living in the country as I do I'm not averse to the mutter of the drums as they sound over the fields without as yet mistaking them for bells. But I can well believe that when they are beaten in narrow city streets the householders cry out like Schopenhauer.

I have asked drummers about this vexed question and they're unanimous in declaring that if there's any illness among their neighbours the drums are immediately silenced. One told me of an incident that happened a few years ago. A man had been sent on the 11th of July night to hang a placard bearing the words 'All bands and drums cease playing at this point' on a lamp-post close to a big hospital. He had just speelied up the post when a voice called 'What are you doing up there?'

'I'm hinging a card up here.'

'Why?'

'To warn the bands that they mustn't play passing the hospital to-morrow.'

'I don't want that card hung there.'

'And who are you?' queried the man up the lamp-post.

'A surgeon at this hospital, and the patients are looking forward to hearing the bands.'

So the card was removed, the man slid down and on the morrow the bands and drums gave of their best passing the hospital.

On the other hand I'm told that in the ancient market town of L—— the drums are beaten without consideration for anyone; young or old, sick or hale. To demur in even the mildest of mild terms against this cannonade being let off under one's bedroom windows is to implant in the minds of these virtuosi a dark suspicion of knavish tricks against the Crown, the Constitution, if not indeed against the very fabric of Christendom itself.

I can't say if this is a true report and I'm reconciled to

remaining in ignorance, for Heaven forfend that I shall ever have to live in the ancient market town of L——.

Although the Hibernian does not chap the big drum to such an extent as the Orangeman yet there are quite a few Hibernian drums in Ulster, particularly in County Armagh. The historical personages painted on the shells are, of course, different. Both organisations wear sashes and carry banners. I need not stress what this happy similarity in regalia (if not in emblems) has meant to the writers of comic Irish tales. To them a rift in the big drum suggests a rift in the intransigency of one side or the other. 'What would happen,' the author asks himself, 'if one band had to borrow from the other?' The answer is pages and pages of rollicking laughter, encouraged by remarks rather like: 'Divil the one o' the Hibs walking on the fifteenth knowed it was King Billy was on the drum ye borrowed from the Orange Lodge. We slapped a coat o' green whitewash on his rid jacket and they all thought 'twas Patrick Sarsfield ridin' to blow up the siege train at Ballyneety!'

I don't know if such incidents ever happened. What you're told in one house is vehemently denied in the next. To pursue the story is like chasing a goat round a hen-house; its tail is always just disappearing round the corner.

But the legend persists. My friend, John MacNeill, the Railway Poet of Whiteabbey, whose memory is much longer than mine, witnessed such an incident and made it into a ballad:

A tale of 'The Twelfth' from the past I recall—
Where it happened I'd better not say:
Old Jimmie McCollum, who lived in the Hall,
Was getting prepared for The Day.
As he rolled out his banner, the Pride of the Land,
With its edging of Orange and Blue;
It tumbled like quicksilver out of his hand
And smash went the side-staffs in two.

As he gazed on the wreck with a look of despair
And he thought of the oncoming morn,
When the Lodge took the road and no banner was there
His soul with reproaches was torn.
In deep gloom he decided in Murphy's to call,
A bottle or two to essay,
When who should step in from the Foresters' Hall
But its keeper, old Charlie M'Stay.

'Say, what ails you, Jimmie, you're white as a ghost
Or a man that has just had a fright!
You look like a jockey that's beat on the post,
What on earth is your trouble to-night?'
Charlie heard his sad tale, then replied with a smile,
'Have a drink and forget all your woe,
Sure I'll fix the thing up in a very short while,
And there's divil the sinner will know.

You have seen our new banner of Emmet the Free?
Well, the staffs are the same as your own,
And I think, on the quiet, between you and me,
You could manage to have them on loan;
For though I belong to a different Church,
And may walk in another parade,
I'm not one to leave an old friend in the lurch,
On account of the tune that is played.

Besides, I'd be mad if that upsetting lot
From the village of Ballymahaff
Should e'er get the laugh on old Ballyslidought
For the sake of a miserly staff.
They're a little bit longer than yours, I would say,
By maybe three inches or more,
So to-morrow when Billy rides out on the grey
He'll be higher than ever before!'

'Well, Charlie, my boy, that's a load off my mind,
But if ever it's known in this place,
By my faith, we will travel as fast as the wind,
With the village behind us in chase!'
'Now, Jimmie man, never meet trouble half way,
'Twill be here soon enough, should it come,
Cheer up and look pleasant, to-morrow's The Day
That you murder the fife and the drum.'

They sat to make sure that they shouldn't be seen,
Till slumber was deep over all.
Then they drew the staffs out of the banner of green,
And carried them down to the Hall,
Where the crafty conspirators argued and wrought
In friendly and bellicose strain,
Till the shimmering banner of Ballyslidought
Swung out in its glory again.

On the Twelfth night when every wearied leg
Had homeward happily rolled,
The staffs were returned from the Orangemen's flag
To the banner of Emmet the Bold.
And the smiling conspirators, glasses in hand,
Voiced a precept that should not offend:
'The best of good luck to our kindly old land,
Where they never go back on a friend!'

That would be a pleasant note to end on but every flute doesn't play the same tune. If these stories persist they persist, as I have said, in the face of vehement denial. William James Connor of Ballyslidought, for example, would have had none of them. When William James was lying on his death-bed he announced his intention to change his religion. His family, understandably, were rather put-out at this vagary. They appealed to the doctor to reason with the old man. 'That's a matter for your clergyman, not for me,' said the doctor.

'Doctor dear,' said they, 'd'ye think we could go near the clergyman with a story like that. That ould fool up-stairs'll make us the laughing-stock of the parish afore he's finished.'

'It's no concern of mine,' said the doctor and went up-stairs. But after he had examined his patient curiosity got the better of him. 'William James,' said he 'what's all this carry-on about changing your religion?'

'I'm for changing it,' said William James stoutly.

'And what will the people in the kitchen below think, and what will all your old friends say?'

'I don't give a damn,' said William James.

'That's a remarkable thing for a man to say who's held so firmly to his principles for over ninety years.'

'Doctor,' said William James, 'speak up like a man and tell me how long I have afore me.'

'William James,' said the doctor, 'you're ninety-three and you haven't spared yourself. I could give you a year, I could give you a month, I could give you a week. That's how it is.'

'I might never rise from this bed?'

'You might never rise from that bed.'

'Then doctor,' said William James, 'isn't it better that one of their sort should die than one of our sort?'

Exaggerated? Of course it is. It could happen all the same.

Chapter Two

ROAMING THE FIELDS ON BOXING DAY

'LET THE HARE SIT,' said the huntsman. It is a phrase of the chase rubbed so smooth that I had always thought it was a proverb. But I heard it used in its pristine sense one needle-sharp Boxing Day in a field outside Tassagh. I had been trailing behind three men as they crept up the ditch that bounded the field. We were looking for a hare and I didn't want to be the one to find it. So I followed at a distance not letting my gaze wander too far on either side. Suddenly the huntsman stopped: 'Let the hare sit,' he said over his shoulder. He must have thought I was on his heels

for his companions didn't need the advice. He crouched and
crept backwards a few steps and then turned. 'I have her
lying!' he crowed and at that moment I saw the hare leave
her den and go away across the field in a precise and beautiful
arc. The man let a great guldher out of him and we heard
the hounds and horns explode from the hollow below the
field in which we stood.

To enjoy a hunt one must presumably either run with the
hare or hunt with the hounds. But there is also a less energetic and indeed if you wish neutral position in which you
can dispose yourself to follow the sport. That is to climb
to a hilltop and watch the hunt

> For as the hare whom hounds and horns pursue
> Pants to the place from whence at first she flew

it is possible by moving from hill to hill to keep the hare
and hounds in view as they sweep the countryside in a
circle—a circle drawn by the hunted animal.

It's no affectation on my part to suggest that the hare
enjoys the hunt. I've been told so by a score of men who
have followed their dogs for two score years through the
fields of Armagh, Tyrone, Fermanagh and Monaghan.
They do not seek the hare's life. Indeed, if he is obviously
flagging the dogs are 'run-off'. But this is not so easy for a
tired hare gives off a heavier scent and the pursuit and cry
of the hounds when they know that their quarry is losing
pace becomes 'wickeder'. It's only in the past few years
when hares have become more plentiful that the huntsmen
have tolerated in the chase that cretin of the canine world,

the greyhound. A shotgun is still the weapon of the barbarian.

Now all this was to me a nuance, for I come from a part of the Province where sportsmen justify hunting in so far as it can be justified by eating what they kill, vermin excepted. (Apart, that is, from some preposterous individuals on horseback who used to arrive in the district with a stag enclosed in a thing like a pantechnicon. This unhappy beast was released and chased across the townland until the 'hunters' had had enough. It was then secured again by underlings and hoisted back into the conveyance and driven away. I have no doubt that the stag enjoyed being hunted. Man's ego makes him remarkably adroit in interpreting animal behaviour.)

Of the many legends connected with the hare the most popular is that of the hare woman. It was known to the Huntsman of King Edward II of England in the fourteenth century:

'I will teach all those who wish to learn hunting as I also have learnt before these hours. Now we will begin with the hare. And why, Sir, will you begin with the Hare, rather than any other beast?

'I will tell you. Because she is the most marvellous beast which is on this earth. And at one time it is male, and at another time it is female.'

I heard a variant of the hare-woman tale from an old man in the Inishowen district of Donegal. 'There was one time,' he said, 'a wee fellow that lived with his granny in a sod house by Carndonagh. And one day two sportsmen came round and two hounds with them. The wee lad was working at the turf beyont the house and the sportsmen came at him. "Young fellow," says one of them, "could you ever rise us a hare?" "No," says the wee lad, "the hares is very scarce about here." "If you can rise us a hare," says the sportsman, "I'll give you ten shillings." Now the wee fellow was mad keen to earn the ten shillings. "Well, wait," says he, "till I ask my granny does she know where there's a hare lying about. So stand yous there till I come back." Well, he was back before he had gone. He took the two men down by a whinny knowe. "Look out for yourselves now and you'll see a race," says he. He had hardly spoke when out pops a hare and the two hounds into it as hard as they could go, up and down, back and forrid. One time as they were passing, the hounds was giving it very tight to the hare and she juked them and threw them off. "Well done, granny!" shouts the wee fellow, "well done, don't let them catch you. Well done, granny!" So the wee fellow's granny got away. She was a witch d'ye see?'

'The whole purpose of the hunt is *not* to kill the hare but to see the hounds working,' the Armagh man will tell you, not without impatience if you persist in thinking that a hare's chief end is *Timbale de Lièvre*.

The stranger, of course, will be unable to appreciate the finer points of the hound-work. Nor will he until he has talked to an experienced hunter be able to appreciate the wiles and stratagems of the hare.

The hounds are usually bred and maintained by farmers who bring them along on the day of the hunt to make the pack. It is this individual ownership which introduced rivalry between the hounds apart from the contest of life

and death between the hounds and the hare. Not only can
the experienced huntsman, out of view but within earshot,
tell how the chase is flowing through the hills, but listening
to the cry of the pack he can tell which hound is hot on the
hare's heels. And so noted hounds have their names
embedded in balladry:

> As they flew over yonder hill
>   It was a lovely sight.
> There was dogs black and yellow
> There was dogs black and white
> The bouncing hare she did her best
>   Upon that frosty ground
> When that great dog from Killileagh
>   Brave Rattler took her down.

I have listened to a brave few of these hunting ballads in
County Armagh pubs and farm-kitchens. Some are old
favourites like Cranagill:

> It being on a Monday morning
> It was on St Patrick's Day
> Sweet music of a hunting-horn
> Blew loudly on yon brae.

But others in the mouth of the singer are as amenable as
calypso to chronicle fresh victories and new champions.
If the singer should lose the scent of his story and fall silent
he is urged by his audience to 'Try back! Try back!'

It is the cry of the huntsman when the hare has outwitted
the hounds and left them fuddled and perplexed on the
border of new terrain. He may have taken to the high road,
though here the keen eye of the hunter can detect the full

track or even the 'nail', a small puncture in the frost or
dust; he may run among sheep

> *For there his smell with others being mingled*
> *The hot scent-snuffling hounds are driven to doubt,*
> *Ceasing their clamorous cry till they have singled*
> *With much ado the cold fault cleanly out;*

He may jink across a fresh-dunged field or bound through
a recently sprayed orchard, easy to come on in the Garden
County of Ireland, where they cloud the trees in nineteen
various sprays between September and April.

Danger deviseth shifts; wit waits on fear. And sympathy
no less presupposes knowledge. I came away from the winter
fields of Tassagh impressed by the enthusiasm and gaiety of
the hunters, but for me much of the attraction of the hunt
remains a cold scent. It appeared nothing more or less than
a small and graceful animal (in Irish the hare is *garrey* or
little deer) pursued by a crowd of men with the best inten-
tions—and a pack of hounds.

★

Many years ago I was in at the death of a custom. Every
Boxing Day the men of our family met to shoot over a
small farm in County Down. It being a custom they came
without invitation. To the man of the house they stood in
the relationship of sons, nephews, cousins, second-cousins,
the children of cousins and second-cousins and in other
variations of tenuous and complicated ties of blood and
marriage all carefully and precisely stored in the memories
of the womenfolk.

About fifteen men gathered at the house with eight guns

between them including the two farm guns. I'm sure about the number of guns for I was at that age when a strange gun was of much more interest than a stranger.

On Christmas Eve a sudden and bitter frost had grasped the countryside, and the following morning its whitened knuckles shone on roofs and trees and rocks. The air was as clear and plangent as crystal glass so that a bark or shot rang over the fields and echoed among the hills like receding footsteps. In the house the kitchen range roared and blew until its rings and orifices glowed poppy-red and scalding water had to be drawn from the brass tap in its hinch. Outside in the close the frozen earth had curled up between the cobbles leaving them sunken in their pits like sightless eyes. I was unable to draw water from the well, and when the man of the house came with a spade to break the ice diamonds glittered in his beard.

But overnight the weather softened and a raw white mist rose out of the small lough three fields away and crept into the hedges and the alders and reeds that fringed the water. The sky was not so much calm as dead. Everything was motionless and the only sounds were the voices of the huntsmen and the susurration of their feet through the dripping grass.

The men tramped slowly across the meadows exchanging gossip and Christmas cigarettes. The young men, who didn't take the hunting very seriously, anticked about laughing and shouting, shouldering each other off the pad and lifting the children on to their shoulders. The older men dandered along at their ease, gun-butts tucked under their arms, the barrels resting on their wrists. Their talk was quiet, even serious, for most of them hadn't met each other for a year. Peace had been declared in the previous month and they recalled companions who had shot over these fields on other Boxing Days.

A shallow burn, the Longstone, wandered down from among the drumlins and ran along the bottom of the field on its way to the lough. We scrambled across the narrow coffin-shaped stone that gave the burn its name. Several men who had straggled away to the left were leaping the burn, their emptied guns held over their heads.

This sodden rush-covered waste bordering the lough was traditionally the turning-point of the shooting party, and on this dreich morning no one felt inclined to go further. The *convention* had been fulfilled for another year, two or three shots had been fired and as everybody agreed, this was not good country for sport.

'I think,' said the son of the house, 'we'll turn. The dinner'll be waiting.' There was a murmur of agreement without betraying, of course, any sign of eagerness.

'We had bad luck to-day,' said the young man.

'Not a word,' cried several of the visitors, 'sure the district's shot out and that's a fact!'

Then in sharp contradiction we heard three shots fired down by the lough. The fusillade startled everyone. Some of the men ran off through the rushes and dank bracken until they had a clear view of the lough. There they stopped abruptly, shouting and gesticulating. I ran after them and by clambering on a fallen alder I could see the surface of the water. A swan was milling round and round in the centre of the lough beating one great wing. 'Look!' shouted a man and pointed. Two figures were clambering up a distant field. 'Who are they?' someone asked. The man narrowed his eyes to assist his memory rather than his sight. 'Those two young fellows from Belfast—Hughie McVeigh's nephews.' The swan, now raising its wing with great effort, was drifting towards the opposite shore. The men around me were murmuring '. . . belong to the King . . . unlawful to shoot . . . royal . . . birds. . . .'

A man plucked off his hat and flung it savagely to the ground. 'The dirty whelps!' he shouted. The young man with all the threads of involved and intricate relationships to keep disentangled held up a deprecating hand. 'Now, now,' he said, 'now, now. . . .'

A big fellow, a neighbour of ours, threw open the breech of his gun and fumbled in his jacket pocket. 'I'll finish it off,' he said. He strode away through the rushes towards the little jetty of corrugated iron from where in the summer the local lads floated out frogs with hooks in their bellies to catch pike.

The corrugated sheet dipped under his weight and sent a tremor through the melting wafer-thin ice. I saw the big man raise his gun and straddle himself steady as the bird floundered into his sights. It took the blast of hail in the hollow between wing and body. A spout of feathers flew up, paused, and idled down to the surface of the reddened water.

That was the last time the men of the family gathered for the Boxing Day shoot. Looking back now, I suspect that the custom had lost its spontaneity many years before. Feathered out by the ritual of hospitality it floated charming but inanimate on the surface of sentiment. It only required the unwitting brutality of two city lads to blow it to fragments.

The Boxing Day shoot still persists in many parts of Ulster, for a custom is myriad-headed and cannot be finished at a thrust; but on that Boxing Day it died on one farm and in time the news of its death idled across a district.

Chapter Three

'I WORK DOWN THE ISLAND'

THE EARLIEST FRAGMENT OF industrial folklore that I remember hearing as a child was supposed to be a description of how the Belfast working-class was employed 'a hundred years ago'—about the time the first shipbuilding yard was raised on the River Lagan. 'The women,' it ran, 'were in the mills, the men were at the street corners, and the children were tethered to the table legs.'

The historian, doubtless, would be mildly amused at such an ingenious description. I've always had a sneaking affection for the run and rhythm of the saying, but one must agree, regretfully, that it is more epigrammatic than accurate.

Even if the menfolk were propping up the gables of Victorian Belfast, it is unlikely that they could have been put to building vessels as easily as their fellows in the countryside were employed in the socially essential task of building 'famine walls' around gentlemen's estates. But there is no need to conjecture on what the first Belfast shipyard meant to the artisans of the town, or rather what the artisans of the town meant to the shipyard. In 1791, William Ritchie, a native of Ayrshire, arrived on the Lagan with ten men and a quantity of shipbuilding gear. He found in Belfast no more than half a dozen jobbing ship carpenters, and these, he tells us, 'being without any person to direct them, were not by that means constantly employed'. In the following half-century shipwrights and engineers from the Clyde and Tyne were to contribute much to the growing prestige of the Belfast shipyards, until, in the 1860s, Edward James Harland could say with pride, 'The men in our employment are mostly of our own training, and the foremen have been promoted from the ranks.'

With over a century and a half of history behind it, I think that it is reasonable, then, to look for custom and tradition in the Belfast shipyard, or the Queen's Island as it has been called for this past hundred years. For into it flow not only all those trades that shape metal with such clangour and dexterity, but the ancient crafts of the rigger, the sailmaker, the carpenter, the woodcarver, the painter, and gilder. While the trades and skills that contribute to the building of a great vessel remain jealously insular, the men who pursue them do not. By their daily proximity customs grow among them. Whatever the idiosyncrasy or ritual may be, it is accepted as authentic tradition, dormant when unemployment empties the slips and shops, remembered and revived when keel plates are laid down once more. So long as it retains significance it extends beyond 'natural recessions' and is remembered by succeeding generations of workers employed in the same industry.

This characteristic is not, of course, peculiar to the Belfast shipyard worker. In his admirable book *The British Worker* Dr Ferdynand Zweig says: 'In my enquiries I came to realise that the past is something still alive and potent, carried on into the present by the habits and customs it engendered. It is handed down from one generation to the next just as myths and folklore are handed down, and sometimes the form it takes is purely mythological. And even more powerfully it lingers on in our subconscious mind, its images vague and, though emotional more than rational, strengthened by their very vagueness. These images deriving from collective experience form a strong though invisible bond between men.' I should add that Dr Zweig is referring not so much to craft customs as to the 'load of bitter memories of the past'. The Belfast shipyard worker of middle-age carries his share of that load, particularly memories of the 'Hungry Thirties'. I remember listening to a journeyman fitter recalling that black time in the history of the Belfast working-class: 'When you were out of a job,' he said 'you got down about fifteen minutes before starting time and took up your position at the gate nearest your department. We called it the "Cattle Market". You always left your pride and dignity at home when you went down to the Cattle Market. Everybody was pushin' so as the foreman would get a good view of you when he came out. It was damnable to hear your mates squabbling among themselves about who was standing in front of who. It was humiliation all right.'

Several times, in conversation with shipyard workers, I've asked them whether they would like to change their jobs. 'Many a time,' said one of them, 'we would like to get out of the 'yard and into the town—just for a change. Anyway, that's what we say and at times we manage it. But you miss the wags, the debates, the discussions, the practical jokes, and of course, your pals. . . .'

And it goes beyond that. *Where* you serve your apprenticeship has much to do with it. As one shipyardman told me: 'The fellow who served his time in the shipyard is usually called a '''yard boy''—it doesn't matter if he's seventy years old, he's always a '''yard boy'', and the fellow who served his time in the building trade—he's called a "townie". Even if he was to work sixty years in the shipyard—he's still a "townie".' And another said: 'There is definitely a distinction made. I had a brother who was a joiner and he served his time in the shipyard and he got his London City and Guilds and that sort of thing. He was considered a very good craftsman. Well, he went out to work in the building trade. He was only there a day; they discovered that he had served his apprenticeship in the shipyard and he got his cards that night.'

But even when a shipyard worker gets a start in a city job there is often a hankering and longing to get back to the 'yard. 'I got fed up with the dirt and noise of the ship-

building,' a painter said, 'so I got a job with a town con-
tractor. He put me to work in an empty house. There I was
all on my own with nobody to talk to but the crows. Three
days of that soon sickened me, especially when I began to
think of my mates down the 'yard. That was enough—the
cards were collected right away and I was soon back on
the old routine.'

'Once a 'yardman always a 'yardman.' Once you've
served your time in the shipyard only a tremendous effort,
or more likely some unforeseen circumstance, will take you
into another job. I risk overstating this point, for the
Islandmen and their families are a distinct and highly
individual community. Their work, their pastimes, their
industrial history separate them in some way from their
fellow citizens. At one time the streets in which they lived,
some of them under the shadow of the tower cranes, were
known as the 'shipyard districts'. Various factors have
contributed to a wider dispersal throughout the city of the
shipyard workers' homes. A boiler-maker said: 'One good
reason for the breaking-up of the old shipyard districts—
although it was a bad one at the time—was the Nazi air-
raids. They cleared out most of the homes, and now, in my
opinion, the shipyard worker on the average is living out
in a far better locality and has a far nicer home. One thing
he needed very badly, and that modern houses have, is a
bathroom; the shipyardman needs that when he comes
home. And he has a bit of a garden now to do a bit of
weeding in and grow some of his own food.'

That was one worker's opinion, and no doubt it was
shared by his wife. But, talking to the wives and mothers

who still live in the traditional shipyard streets, I found a
strong feeling of community evident. 'We're just one big
family.' 'We all live together and we try to help one
another.' 'If one sleeps in and the other is up you go and
rap them, and that kind of thing. We're really that close
together we can do nothing else.'

In such a close-knit community the day-to-day com-
panionship among the men doesn't end with the knocking-
off whistle. In the evenings they meet in their own clubs,
usually held over public-houses. Some of these clubs, such
as the Welders' Club, are more or less restricted to the
journeymen and apprentices who follow the same trade.
The Cork Clubs are a feature of the shipyard districts.
They meet once a week in the local pub where the gathering
is presided over by Cork Chairman assisted by Cork
Secretary and Cork Treasurer. When the club is in session
a large 'King Cork' sits on the table in front of the Chairman.
The 'King Cork' is cork only by courtesy for it is usually
a piece of ordinary wood turned on a lathe and decorated
with colours of a football club. The 'King Cork' plays an
important part in these gatherings. When it is placed on the
table the club is in session and the members are subject to
the rules of the constitution which are firmly, and genially,
enforced by the Chairman. The rules are simple and are
mainly intended to ensure good-fellowship and good
entertainment at the same time permitting some small
concession to ritual. Each member on entering the room
touches the Master Cork with a beer cork, his badge of
membership, which he is expected always to carry with him.
If he can't produce this badge on being challenged by

another member, he pays a fine on the next club evening. Here are a few rules picked at random from the membership card:

All members when entering Clubroom must touch King Cork with Cork; failing to do so, fined 1d.

Meetings to commence at 7.45 p.m. sharp. Any member late without a reasonable excuse to be fined the sum of 6d. After 8.45 p.m. 9d.

Any member using the word Cork on Sunday, fined 3d.

Any member failing to produce Cork when asked by another member, fined 3d.

Any member using obscene language when asked for Cork, fined 1d.

Any member found with two Corks to be expelled.

Any member not singing when asked, fined 6d.

The regulations are simple, childish if you like. But to say that and say no more would be completely to misunderstand the atmosphere of a Cork Club. Most of the members are keen, some of them militant, trade unionists, with a thorough knowledge of trade union procedure. All of them, from the 'old hand' to the youngest apprentice, have, in varying degrees, a jealous pride in the customs and privileges of their craft. The rules of the Cork Clubs, with their rudimentary humour, are a deliberate reaction from this sterner discipline; a straightforward procedure to ensure a pleasant and convivial evening among workmates. Provided he likes a song and a bit of crack, the visitor who is fortunate enough to be invited along to a Cork Club night will enjoy himself from the moment he's pressed to name his fancy and the drink board bearing the inscription

23 pints porter
9 bots. stout
1 bot. lemonade

is sent rattling down the service hatch to the eager curate
below in the public bar.

★

There can be few occupations, outside agriculture, where
the woman of the house knows more about the day-to-day
work of her menfolk than shipbuilding. 'I've a husband
and two sons working on the —— Castle,' a housewife told
me, 'and I could name you every alleyway and room in that
boat without having put my foot in her.'

Like the womenfolk of most workers in heavy industry,
the shipyard workers' wives are cheerful and pugnacious
folk, not very interested in the rest of their fellow-citizens,
bound together as they are in neighbourliness, and sharing
common problems such as the fear of unemployment in
the 'yard or accidents.

It has been said that 'the accidents accompanying shipbuilding brought fame to the surgeons of Belfast as surely
as Edinburgh's dirt and overcrowding made Lister's name
famous'.* In spite of the most ingenious safeguards and
precautions, danger is always at the shipyard worker's
elbow. A painter said to me: 'Sometimes you wonder why
the accident rate isn't higher; it speaks well for the men
themselves that this isn't so. A few years in the 'yard and
you develop a kind of sixth sense, a feeling of danger that
always puts you on your guard.' And when safeguards and

* Dr E. Estyn Evans, *Belfast, the Site and the City*.

intuition fail, and a man is injured, sympathy doesn't hang around waiting on prudence. A subscription list is opened among his mates in shop or boat 'to put the bad times over'. If he has been killed or so badly injured that it is unlikely that he will ever return to work, his tools are auctioned among his fellow-workers at prices much higher that the men would usually pay for second-hand tools, and the money is sent to their old workmate's family.

The shipyard worker's wife, because things might be worse, is always ready to tell a good story when things aren't so bad. 'My husband come in one night,' a New-townards Road woman said, 'and I thought his cap was sitting awful funny on his head. I says "what's wrong with your head?" and he lifts off his cap and shows me a great big lump on it. He had a bandage on his finger and I says "what's wrong with your finger?" Well, he took his torch out—he must carry a torch y'see—and it was all bashed. I says, "in the name of goodness what happened to you?" "Ach," says he, "there was a man thonder and I was showing him how to do a job, and he missed the job and hit me on the head. Next time he missed the job and hit me on the finger, and the next time he missed the job and hit the flashlight and flattened it." Says I, "what did you do then?" Says he, "well, I just threw him out and did the job myself".' She paused and added, 'Of course he isn't always as patient as that.'

★

In a shipyard, boys do the work of men and men do the work of giants. In the Queen's Island they still talk of the worker who drove over three thousand rivets in nine working hours. To-day, the riveter is giving way to the welder, and the journeyman painter who laid coat upon coat of glass-smooth paint on bulkheads now swings a paint-gun. Some of the men regret the change and say that it has resulted in a deterioration of craftsmanship. One journeyman said to me: 'I remember getting advice from an old painter one time. He asked me why I came to the trade and I told him that I had an ability for drawing. Says he sadly, "Son, the only thing worth drawing down here now, is your wages".' But most of the younger tradesmen, particularly those who have worked a spell in cross-channel yards, are inclined to be impatient with this attitude. To them the vessels that leave the slips in the Queen's Island are still the best examples of shipbuilding in the world, 'built to wear out the ocean'.

But my concern is not with the ships but with the men who build them. And the 'old hands' in the 'yard talk about the changes they have seen in the shipyard workers' homes, clothing and diet. 'There's been great changes in this dozen years,' a joiner remarked: 'but I've seen greater in my working life. When I went to serve my time, sixty years ago, the craftsmen at that time came to work dressed in a frock coat and a castor hat. At that time each journeyman had a tool chest about three feet long and nearly two feet wide with a recess at the back. In that recess he kept his long white apron and his white linen cap—just exactly like what chefs wear nowadays. When he arrived in the morning he took off his frock coat and his castor hat, put on the apron and the cap, and laid the coat and hat in the recess until going-home time. Now that was the common dress sixty years ago of the old cabinet-makers and joiners and carpenters.'

I've seen one or two of these tool chests; lovely pieces of carpentry decorated with sailing vessels and steamships in mother-o'-pearl inlay. They were probably the last few in existence, for most of them were destroyed in the air-raids of 1941. Other trades were distinguished by some characteristic touch in dress. The riggers were originally sea-going men who occasionally took a month or so ashore and worked in the nearest shipyard. For generations afterwards their dry-land descendants wore the round woollen cap of the mariner. For the engineers or fitters it was the deep-sea glazed peak cap. The riveter dressed in moleskins tied below the knee with 'yorks', and in his leisure hours he wasn't counted a good riveter 'unless he had a black silk scarf and owned a whippet'.

When 'yorks' were in fashion, most Islandmen carried their midday meal or 'piece' wrapped in a red pocket handkerchief. To-day they carry their food in a tin lunch-box, those of them, that is, who don't eat at the canteens. There is a distinct cleavage of opinion as to whether the Islandman should buy his midday meal in the canteen or boil his wee black can and eat his piece at the bench or in the 'dugout'. The traditionalists are all for the wee black can. They maintain 'that once everybody starts going to the canteen the shipyard character becomes extinct'. For the lunch-hour is of great importance to the shipyard worker. In that forty minutes an involved pattern of discussions, bargains, auctions, gospel-meetings, competitions and

leagues is carried through from year to year, even in some
of the old-fashioned games from lifetime to lifetime.

'One of the first things I remember in serving my time,'
a fitter told me, 'was the choice of schools that I could go to
during the meal hour. I could go to the card school, or I
could go to the Bible class, or I could go to the debating
classes on politics—and I may say I tried them all and
benefited from them all.'

These groups gather at the benches or in the 'dugouts',
a word bequeathed by the shipyardmen who came back
from the 1914-18 War. Here the apprentice learns the
minutiæ of shipyard tradition: that he must buy a pound
or two of boiling sweets for his mates out of his first pay-
packet; that he must not clod bolts at the seagulls for are
they not old fellow-workmen, joiners, painters, boiler-
makers and plumbers, loath to leave the scene of their
earthly labours?

★

It has been said that *quiz*, one of that great tribe of
hardworking words of doubtful parentage, was, in fact,
fathered by an eighteenth-century Irish theatre manager.
He made a bet that he could introduce a new word into the
language within twenty-four hours. That night he had his
novel and grotesque word chalked on walls all over Dublin,
and by the next day the citizens were speculating on its
meaning. The inventiveness of that Smock Alley wit is
inherited by the Islandman and he announces the birth of
his conceit in the same manner—by chalking it on walls.
Belfast folk still recall the meteoric passage of Big Aggie's

Man through the affairs of the city, and indeed, of the Province. He brooded over the deliberations at Stormont, raised hell in the City Hall, brought in 100-1 winners, refereed football matches with a heart-warming partiality, partnered ten thousand lonely spinsters, was identified, amid delighted chuckles, on the fringe of Society wedding groups, and had a finger in every accident, cantrip, and stroke of luck that could befall a Belfast working-class family.

Through the years Big Aggie's Man has had a number of lesser successors, some dimly remembered, most forgotten. The last, I think, was Skiboo. But Skiboo lacked the gusto, the diversity of his great predecessor. Furthermore, the origin of Big Aggie's Man remains shrouded in impenetrable mystery. The creator of Skiboo, overcome by his momentary inspiration, revealed himself. The BBC and the Press tracked him down and interviewed him in the shipyard. On the next morning nothing has ever been quite so dead as was Skiboo.

For me it will always be Big Aggie's Man. But oh, that we had had a Richard Strauss to set down, to the last demi-semi-quaver, that antic career!

Chapter Four

THE WAY TO CATCH THE MOUNTAIN DEW

'WOULD YOU AGREE THAT the Irish are much addicted to the drinking of whiskey?'

The answer to that question posed one hundred years ago by Lord Monteagle of Brandon, chairman of one of the many Select Committees sent over periodically to examine the life and good times of the Irish landlord and his tenantry, was of course in the affirmative.

A hundred years ago, just as to-day, there were many Irishmen who never lipped strong drink, but Select Committees by their very nature are commissioned to fix their

Cyclops eye on what they want to see and no more. Indeed, if that was all their Lordships wanted to know they could have sat comfortably at home and found the answer in the mission of Father Matthew or the novels of William Carleton.

'The blood of every prolific nation is naturally hot, but when that hot blood is inflamed by ardent spirits it is not to be supposed that men should be cool; and God, He knows, there is not on the level surface of this habitable globe a nation that has been so thoroughly inflamed by "ardent spirits" as Ireland.'

Carleton the Tyrone peasant knew his countrymen. In *The Faction Fight* and *Larry McFarland's Wake* the ominous drumbeat of that phrase 'God, He knows' runs through the terrible descriptions of the Irish peasantry in liquor.

But Carleton knew why his neighbours, a people barely suffered in their own glens and hills, drank until they drowned the memories of yesterday and fears of the morrow. And from that knowledge sprang his pity and anger. If we were never to open another book on the conditions of the Irish peasantry in the eighteenth and nineteenth centuries Carleton's tales would be sufficient to make the accompanying ribaldries of *Phiz* with their apish long-lipped clowns as false and ineffectual as *graffiti* on a lavatory wall.

By the eighteenth century the distilling of poteen had become a highly organised activity involving the inhabitants over wide districts. Even the vagrants of the road knew when they were expected and what they were expected to do. A witness testifying before the Monteagle Committee remarked, 'The stills are always made by travelling tinkers; whenever you see those fellows about you may suspect something.'

As for the spirit itself, no one seems to be quite sure when it was first distilled in Ireland. There is a recipe for *usquebagh* in the seventh century Red Book of Ossory. *Usquebagh* was a compound liquor and the recipe demands mace, cloves, cinnamon, ginger, coriander-seed, cubebs, raisins, liquorice, sugar and 'saffron, well-dissevened and put into a linen cloth, and hung at the worm's end; whereby all the tincture will be extracted and run amongst the distilled goods'. These aromatics were not gathered from the gardens of Ireland but from the pharmacopœia of the East.

It is plain then that *usquebagh* and whiskey are not synonymous although Dr Johnson was of an opposite opinion. '*Usquebagh*,' he says, 'is an Irish or Erse word which signifies the "water of life".' It is a compounded distilled spirit, being drawn on aromatics; and the Irish sort is particularly distinguished for its pleasant and mild flavour. The Highland sort is somewhat hotter, and by corruption in Scotch they call it 'whisky'.

The Irish stillers have been pursued as assiduously by the story-tellers as they were by the police. And always with an ear cocked for a laugh. But the stiller never operated his clandestine engine for the joke of it, or the thrill, or even cheap liquor for a frolic. In a society where the cottier farming six or ten acres of indifferent soil was as likely as not to open a bare cupboard in the morning, the liquor he made on the mountain was made to be sold. The purchasers were strong farmers and agents buying for the gentry 'who had a fancy, a sort of pride in saying to their guests "I can give you a drop of the mountain dew".'

So skilful were the poteen-makers in concealing their stills, and so often did they outwit their pursuers, that the police kept a census of the crops grown in remote and mountainous districts. They claimed knowledge of every diamond and rig of corn or barley and how the cottier disposed of his crop. But it couldn't have been a very effective check on illicit distilling for even in the primitive state of agriculture in the early nineteenth century an acre of oats would yield about ten hundredweights while a gallon of spirit could be produced from only two stones of grain.

Bad harvest weather or a poor crop, not uncommon in a country with an annual rainfall of forty to fifty inches and over sixty inches in the mountainous regions, meant an increase in poteen-running. The only hope that a small farmer had to save anything from his damaged grain was to malt it for distilling. A gallon of poteen made from two stones of grain would fetch, at an average, 4/6. He would be lucky to get 1/6 in the grain market for the same quantity. And the 'grains' or refuse from the still was of great value for cattle-feed, particularly in a district where hay or grazing was hard to come by.

On fair days many a sleek beast was driven out of a rocky glen—a glen with no more feeding in it than the back of your hand, and the sergeant could do no less than return the genial *how-are-ye* of the drover.

Not only broken weather but broken roads encouraged farmers in remote districts to convert their grain. The easy

journey that the farmers of Down and Antrim had to the
Belfast cornmarket meant that there was little or no stilling
in those counties compared to Tyrone, Derry or Donegal.

★

Some years ago I had to stay overnight in a small country
town. Earlier in the day I had met a man called (shall we say?)
Finlay. By the time we had our business completed it was
midday and Finlay, who farmed at the mountain-foot some
miles out, decided to accept my invitation to lunch in the
local hotel.

We made a detour by the bar where, sympathetically, the
conversation turned to liquor and eventually poteen-
making. (We had no eavesdropper, for the barman was a
supernumerary waiter at meal hours and his return was
always announced by a volley of abuse and counter-abuse
as he passed the kitchen-door.) Although Finlay, at first,
tried to be rather offhand not to say second-hand in his
comments it soon became evident that his knowledge of
stilling was more than could be picked up in cross-roads
chatter. He was too opinionated in his criticisms of methods
and materials; too particular and subtle in his explanations.

Then the barman came back to tell us there were two seats
available. During the imported mutton and tinned peas
Finlay was preoccupied. As the rice and raisins were set
before us he leaned across the table and said, under the
chatter of the commercial gentlemen who surrounded us,
'would you like to see a still?' 'Sure,' I replied. We declined
the tea and digestive biscuits and went out to Finlay's jeep.

Most of the darkening afternoon was spent round the

farmhouse and farm. But the sky was still no darker than pewter when two men with a sheepdog entered the close. Finlay told me to put on my trench coat and gave me a thick pair of socks and a pair of rubber boots. As we left the farmhouse I said, 'As clear as this?' After all, I was cast for the part of the novice in this adventure. Finlay smiled gently. 'It'll be dark enough before all's through,' he said.

The two men were day-labourers on the farm. They made no comment on my being there. Finlay, I suppose, had more to lose than they had. We all got into the jeep including the dog.

Before we had rounded the mountain it was dark. We left the secondary road and started to climb. At a fork in the limestone track a scattering of sheep shimmered beyond the dyke. Finlay stopped the jeep and the two men and the dog alighted. I heard them calling on the dog as we drove away. About half a mile further on and up Finlay stopped again and we got out. 'Now,' he said, 'for a bit of climbing.' I followed him into the darkness. He had picked a not-so-dry torrent bed to climb the escarpment. After about ten minutes scrambling I wished that I had decided to ruin my shoes. Even with the added bulk of the woollen socks the borrowed boots fitted infrequently and painfully.

Not a moment too soon for me, Finlay struck out of the ravine to the right. We were on a broad gallery on the mountainside, still sloping violently, but we could walk upright here. I felt the regular rise and fall of ridged earth under my boots. Somewhere in that dripping desolation, I expect, I would have found the tumbled gable of a cottage. The open ground petered out and we were back among the ling and rocks. We must have moved a considerable way round the mountain for the black contour above us had quite changed in shape since we left the ravine. Then before us, I could see, not so much a glow as a thinning of the darkness at ground level. It might have been no more than the wet face of limestone not yet subdued by the night. But it was man-made light and the men who made it were our companions with the sheepdog who had left us at the fork below the mountain. I stumbled over the low turf wall around a shallow pit and warmed my hands indiscriminately at the various receptacles it contained.

I **had** never seen a still before, but recalling photographs of some of the queer contraptions seized by the police this seemed a remarkably well-constructed apparatus. The glow came from a pressure stove burning with a muted roar under the largest container, a creamery can. 'That's where the wash is,' said Finlay.

'Second run,' said one of the farmhands solidly pumping the stove two or three times.

Finlay corrected, nodded. 'That's right—second run. The "doublins" as some folk call it. This'll be the third run—the finished article as you might say.'

'You could still call it the wash,' said the second farmhand from the shadows.

'You could,' agreed his mate straightening from the stove, 'but you don't want to confuse the man.'

Once under way stilling is a leisurely occupation, so they had time to explain what was going on. In Finlay's opinion the pressure stove was an inestimable benefit to the craft of poteen-making. For the first time the stiller had control over his source of heat. In former days, when the wash threatened to boil over, the stiller had either to upset the brew with cold water or douse the fire. When a small quantity of wash was being run off there was always the possibility of the empty metal becoming too hot, singeing the wash, and so spoiling the run. Finlay had avoided this mischance by suspending a chain from the lid of the wash-container to within an inch or so of the bottom. The action of the boiling liquid kept this chain revolving and stirring all the time.

The lid of the creamery can was neatly drilled and a screw-fitting welded on for the attachment of the pipe and worm. The precious vapour rode along this pipe into the coils of the worm suspended in the cooling system, an old oil drum fed from a sluggish trinket that flowed from the scrawbog further up the mountain.

The tail of the worm protruded about a foot from the drum, presumably to help condensation. Under this they had cocked a two-quart glass jug.

'Do they always give poteen three runs?'

'*We* always give ours three runs,' said Finlay.

'There are some who don't?'

'I've seen men drink the singlings—the first run. They did it out of greed not ignorance. Damn good stillers some of them were in their day—'

'Dead?'

'Oh, as doornails.'

I crouched in the corner of the pit and debated whether it was all worth while. I had to take into account the prejudicial fact that my feet were now so cold that I could no longer feel the chafing. But Finlay and his helpers, that is to say the stillers, were at no more discomfort than if they had been following their legitimate business of rounding-up sheep. There was the satisfaction of evading or rather disobeying the law, for if the distilling of illicit liquor is carried on in a hole-and-corner fashion the process itself is a deliberate application of patience, industry and skill. It seemed a much less squalid transgression than that of the greengrocer who overcharges the harassed housewife for vegetables. The penalty for stilling is of course much heavier; not to protect the citizen against alcoholism but to protect the Revenue. The point was neatly made during the taking of evidence at the Monteagle Select Committee. A Mr Golding Bird, Collector of Inland Revenue at Londonderry, when asked to explain the revenue decrease in 1841-42 gave it as his opinion that it was 'due to the work of Father Matthew. The people at that time were largely taking the pledge, and the demand for spirit was lessened; that is the only way I can account for it.' The British Government reduced the duty from 3/8 to 2/8, the consumption of liquor in Ireland rose by 4,189,000 gallons and the Revenue Commissioners were solaced by an increase of £314,000.

The first bead of the liquor swelled at the end of the worm and dropped into the jug. One of the farmhands lowered the sullen roar of the stove and we became aware of the listening darkness around us. Finlay hunkered down over the jug and examined it critically.

'How much do you hope to get?' I asked.

'There was nearly ten gallons of "doublins" put in. I'm looking for the best part of a gallon and a half of spirits.'

The flow accelerated to a falling chain of crystal drops mounting slowly in the jug.

'That'll take time.'

'Ah, you'd be surprised.'

The two helpers joined Finlay. They were obviously pleased with what they saw. I suppose no matter how often a stiller does this sort of thing he never loses the feeling of having triumphantly completed a task in which there was an element of antagonism even treachery in his circumstances, materials, tools. Morality apart, it is a different satisfaction than that of having reaped and stooked a five-acre field. There the difficulties may be anticipated, here the fortuitous must be overthrown and turned to advantage. In a crowd, distilling could pass as an art.

The jug filled and was replaced appropriately by a stone jar. The second farmhand was very circumspect with a small electric torch.

'What happens to it now?' I asked.

'This lot—or most of this lot—will go into a sherry wood cask.'

'And how long will it stay there?'

'A year—maybe two. It depends on when it's wanted. If I'm asked for a drop I syphon it off.'

'Syphon it off?'

Finlay laughed. 'Where this cask is that's the only way to get it out.'

The sheepdog appeared out of the darkness, padded along the low turf wall and disappeared again.

'Gettin' restless,' said the second farmhand. 'She could do with a touch more heat there, Finlay. Just what you would

know.' Finlay knelt at the stove and the flame turned a
more transparent blue behind the wind-shield.

I could follow the progress of the distillation in the glass
jug but not in the stone jar. I began to feel fed-up with the
proceedings. Then the first farmhand began to tap and
knock and listen at the creamery can. He probed the warm
metal with his fingers. He tapped it with his knuckles and
put his ear close to listen to the resonance. He had the
knowing anticipation of a doctor tapping a patient's trunk.
'That's her now,' he said.

Finlay turned out the stove and drew it from under the
washcan. We were left in darkness until the second farmhand let the light from the torch leak out through a lumi-
nous crevice of his fingers. Finlay eased away the mouth
of the jar and replaced it when he saw that the trickle of
spirit still ran freely. 'Will you two boys clear up?' he asked.

The first farmhand nodded. Then 'try her again,' he said.
Finlay took the jar away and we saw that the trickle had
died to reluctant drops lingering, swelling and falling on
the ground. The first farmhand caught a few in his hand.
'Hold the torch here,' he said. He rubbed his hands briskly
together and opened them to show me a light froth on one
palm. 'That's quality for ye,' he said to me with a wink.

'You can manage?' asked Finlay buttoning his jacket.

'Sure,' they replied. Finlay and I left the pit and recrossed
the rough ground until we came to the old ridged cultiva-
tion. Finlay stopped and pointed into the darkness. 'There's
a bit of an old house there. That's where we would have
been to-night if those two eejits had attended to the roof a
month ago, when I told them. They let two or three of

the couplings fall in. But they'll fix it. I'll need it for the sheep-shearing in May.'

'Did people live and work up here as high as this?' I asked as I stumbled along behind him.

He stopped again. 'Man, they did.' He waved his arm in the gloom. 'There's not a dip or rock or bush on this mountainside that hasn't a name. How d'ye explain that? Because this land was worked up to the 500-foot level and above it, that's the reason. There's tumbled gables all round this hill.'

'Was it a decent class of land?'

'It would take three acres to graze a gander.'

'And what happened to the people?'

'They went at the Famine.' He paused. 'And now the only living creature you'll get up here is the sheep, or the hare or the hoody crow—'

'—and an occasional midnight visitor.'

Finlay chuckled and lowered himself into the ravine.

As we bumped and lurched down the mountain I asked about our two companions. 'We'll meet them down here at the fork.'

'I expected that. What would they be doing now?'

'They're putting away the still and getting rid of the wash.'

'Into the wee burn?'

'No, Sir! You don't want that stuff spreading any further than you can help. They'll bury it.'

'And what about the still?'

'She'll be cleaned and dumped behind a sheugh.'

'Until the next time?'

'Indeed, no! She'll be lifted first thing in the morning and stored. You never know who's wandering about up there. Mebbe just a lot of weans picking bilberries but better sure than sorry.'

The jeep creaked and jolted for another hundred yards or so, brushes of whin beating at the sidelights.

'You don't mind me asking these questions?'

'Not at all. Ask your fill.'

'Well, what will you do with that poteen? It's between the three of you, isn't it?'

'Och aye, but we don't take that side of it very seriously. It'll go into cask until I think it's ready. Then whoever wants a drop gets a drop.'

'You keep it for a ceilidhe, maybe?'

'Damn the fears! I wouldn't put that stuff into the hands of a lot of fellows at a ceilidhe! The news would be round the parish by the next morning! Some ould fellow living his lone would get a drop, or I might slip a glass or two into my pocket if I was going to a house where there's a death or some young one going to America. I'd take the man of the house into the back room and give him a sup, mebbe one or two other ould fellows. Grief's always drouthy, you know. But no comment, no talk, not a word said.'

'You never sell it?'

'Never! I've found out that if you give a fellow a drop and make an obligement of it he keeps his mouth shut; if you ask him two or three bob he goes round bumming and blasting to all his friends about his "contacts"—'

'. . . who has a sort of fancy in saying to his friends "I can give you a drop of the mountain dew".'

'Aye, that's a name for it, "Mountain Dew".'

We stopped at the fork where the two farmhands and the dog had left us. There was no sign of them as yet. I gave Finlay a cigarette and lit one myself.

'Two or three bob doesn't seem much for even a small quantity of it.'

'Ah, that's only a token. You wouldn't know what to charge. You couldn't be paid for making the stuff. There was a fellow round here eight or nine years ago went into it for the money. He got rid of it to an eejit of a publican that mixed it with rum. And of course it happened. Two or three young galoots got a tightener of it at a dance. And believe me, when you've got a tightener on poteen no sergeant thinks you've been at the kali-water. The next day they lifted your man, still and all. No, it's no cop.'

I suddenly realised that I had been an accessory, no matter how innocent, to a piece of law-breaking. How could I have explained myself? That I was there just for the fun of the thing? I could see the sergeant's face. I rather wished that this excursion was ended! 'Well, thank God, there were no police about to-night.'

'No, there would have been none of them in that locality to-night.'

'Never go up there I suppose—'

'Oh, I'm sure Sergeant Toal wishes he had a quid for every time he's dandered over the mountain. Been up there shooting with me many's a time.'

I waited. 'They had a bit of business on in the town to-night,' said Finlay.

'Trouble?' I asked, relieved.

'Oh, b'God, I hope not. Just a wee job to keep them all occupied for the evening.' He suddenly switched on the engine. 'Here are the boys—'

The two farmhands with the dog at their heels came clambering over the low dyke. I had a fellow-feeling for that dog. She and I, in our diverse ways, had endured much in common during the past four hours.

We drove back to the farm where we had supper and I exchanged Finlay's boots for my own shoes. Then he offered to drive me back to the town and I shook hands with the two farmhands and bade them goodnight.

'What do they call those fellows?' I asked as we set off.

'Arthur and Joe,' said Finlay. 'Why?'

'Nothing. I was just wondering.'

Finlay whistled a tune under his breath and beat time on the steering-wheel with his hand.

'Not a mute out of you about to-night?'

'Now, need you ask?' This from me in a rather pained voice. After that he settled down to the driving.

'You'll look us up when you're in this part of the world again?'

I promised I would and I've done so on many occasions since.

As we drew up at the hotel Finlay took a 12-oz. bottle full of liquid as clear as spring water from the car pocket and gave it to me. 'There's a drop of medicine for you and make sure where you are before you start the dose.'

'I accept it as an obligement.'

'Aye, that's the play,' said he laughing, and drove off.

As I hirpled painfully into the hotel the barman-boots-waiter was just about to climb the stairs carrying a tray with tea and biscuits.

'I thought you were at the dance?' said he.

'What dance?'

'Ah, there's no end of entertainment in the town the night, sir. There's a dance in the Orange Hall and another in the Foresters! First time in twenty years they've fell on the same night!'

Not only the Church but the State has had to lick its wounds before overcoming a vibrant and living custom. The people do not understand (or else understand too well) the expediency that has made it necessary to decide that what was the ordinary is now the illicit. One of the disadvantages under which the Revenue authorities worked was the stubborn conviction of the country people that they were being unreasonably restrained from converting by their own labour their own crops into a profitable article. Many of them, living on five or ten acres, were rack-rented almost out of existence, and the stilling was a means of livelihood.

Among the procession of landowners, civil servants and Revenue officers that passed before the Monteagle Committee was Head-Constable John Mullarchy. He had this to say: 'If there is an outrage against life or property we would get information from the respectable portion of the community; but as regards illicit distilling we get no advice; they take it as a matter of course.' Lord Monteagle: 'They do not consider it a moral offence?' Head-Constable Mullarchy: 'They do not.'

The stillers considered any subterfuge justified. Revenue officers were delayed, led astray or kidnapped and held until the run was completed and the liquor sold. One still-hunter 'was even obliged by way of humiliation to assist in the working of a still; while, like another Tantalus, the cup of pleasure was held to his parched lips, without the liberty of gratifying his thirsty desires.' Others less fortunate were dropped into bog holes.

The grain being ripe and the moon in the right quarter the stillers would stage a mock faction fight at a fair to hold the police. If by ill-chance they were discovered, the still was carried away by a strong runner a mile or so across the mountain roads where he would be relieved by an accomplice and he by a third until by the morning the still (and the evidence) would be on the other side of the county.

Even when the police laid hands on the poteen the skirmish, so far as the stillers were concerned, was still open to fortune. A story is told in the North Sperrins of three Revenue officers who came on a small keg of poteen concealed in an outhouse. The farmer and his sons had disappeared so the officers carried the keg down to the nearest village. There they found that the village hackney driver had gone off with his long car to 'a funeral, or it might be a wedding'. No one, of course, knew where the event was being solemnised and the officers had to put up at the village tavern until the following morning when they could join the Derry Mail. They were long-headed boys and not prepared to take chances with their prize. They carried the keg up to their sleeping apartment and ordered their supper to be served there. As the officers disappeared upstairs two or three young fellows slipped into the tavern kitchen and held a whispered conversation with the girl preparing the meal. Some money changed hands. She carried the food upstairs and returned to the kitchen. 'It's there,' she said pointing to the ceiling, 'betwixt the fire cheek and the dure and sitting three boords out from the wall.' The stillers pierced the ceiling, the floorboards and the bottom of the keg with a belly-brace and drained the liquor off into a bucket. The Revenue officers found the going pretty easy, no doubt, to the Derry coach.

The stillers were often betrayed by the odour from the boiling wash. In their efforts to douse the sweet penetrating smell they burned bog-fir or tarred boards. A County Derry tinsmith of my acquaintance was warned by the police that he was committing a nuisance by burning old bicycle tyres on his kitchen range. Apart from the scare that this gave him the rubber was in his opinion an excellent and easily controlled fuel under the wash-container. A family of stillers were alleged by the police to have planted clumps of night-scented stock, *Matthiola bicornis*, around their cottage, an imaginative ruse that deserved greater success. But like the peppermint-scented breath, the dissembling odours only drew attention to what they were meant to conceal.

Finlay was solidly of the opinion that the police were trained to recognise the smell given off by the boiling wash. 'I remember a man telling me that they have special courses in the barracks where they taste and smell all classes of liquors. It's all part of a very rigorous training of course, but the law—'

'Look, Finlay' (there's nothing your Ulsterman likes better than dashing away with the flat irony, the flatter and more outrageous, the better) 'can you really smell it at a distance?'

'Sure, if you let the wash get singed. There'll always be a bit of a reek of course. In the nature of things that can't be avoided. But you can take precautions.'

'For example?'

'Let your grain germinate—or "streck" nice and slowly on an earth floor. Then dry it properly at the kiln, or if you have an inquisitive sergeant, do it in handfuls on the griddle at home. When you have it beetled down and mixed with your warm water, and your yeast put in, wait till it's "watery silent"—all the fizz gone out of it. Do it all at walking pace. When you have it in the still don't blaze up your heat because you're in a hurry and you'll avoid a stink in more senses than one. Hasten slowly and you won't meet sorrow. That's the best of your play,' concluded Finlay.

'I'll be careful,' said I involuntarily.

Chapter Five

RESPECT THE GOOD NEIGHBOURS

IN JUNE 1951 THE BBC in Northern Ireland decided to explore the region for any fairy lore that might still linger in the glens and mountainsides. Michael J. Murphy, the Ulster folklorist, was commissioned to carry out the preliminary survey. The amount of material that came in from Murphy as he combed the countryside surpassed anything that we had expected. It also became evident from the ages of the story-tellers that the exploration had started none too early.

Then in November, when he had completed his last

report, we set out with recording equipment to retrace his journey. We worked over Northern Ireland district by district, the Mournes, the Sperrins, South Armagh, the Glens of Antrim with sallies to the Braid Valley, the Fintona district, the shores of Strangford and Lough Erne. Although such a short time had passed since Michael J. Murphy's first visit we were met here and there by a padlocked door or a slow shake of the head. Some old man or woman had taken a grandfather's stories to the graveyard.

But fortunately most of our story-tellers were alive and well and, expecting us, had dipped deep in memory. Not all of them of course were quite so willing to give us what they had found there. We met men and women who could hardly tell their stories for laughter, but we politely stared the laughter out of face and got the story. There were others who glanced quickly out at the fields and said 'This is Tuesday, their heels are to me and they won't hear me', and thus safeguarded sat down to tell us of the ark of meal that never ran out, the light dancing in the thorn—'we would pass it on our way home'—and the morning that the grandfather came in white and shaking and whistling a tune unknown to any fiddler in that district. Then there were the few old men who would have kept us cracking at the hearth all night but had a dozen good reasons for not talking about the Good Neighbours.

I have set down here—with the minimum of comment— some of the stories as they were told to me.

Did our story-tellers believe in fairies? They were mostly seventy years of age and upward; but they were not as old as the whitethorn bush their grandfather feared as a child.

Doubt the story and they showed you the thorn; doubt the
thorn's age whence came the story? The question of *belief*
then did not enter into the matter. A great number of
the tales were family history and therefore, so far as
we were concerned, incontrovertible. Most of these tales
and experiences had never been seen in print by the story-
tellers and yet men and women who couldn't find each
other's district on a map could have repeated their story in
chorus.

We found the same repetition in the description of *skeags*
or fairy thorns, the malicious changelings (one old man
glaring across the hearth swore his sister was one), the
lochery-man with the gillicup of gold who threw snuff in
his captor's eyes, and of course the magnificent fairy halls
under the raths full of dancing 'and all classes of joviality'. We
got a hundred tributes to the sweetness of fairy music and
recalled what St Patrick said when he listened to the harping
of Cascorach the Fay: 'Good indeed it were but for a twang
of the fairy spell that infests it; barring which nothing could
more nearly than it resemble Heaven's harmony!'

How did the Fairy Race come to Ireland? There is of
course the story of an ancient race being driven into the
underground places of the earth by invaders; the Formorians
by the Tuatha Da Danaan and they in turn by the Milesians.
These dispossessed, haunting the caves and subterranean
chambers and remote islands of the West, became the
Sluagh Sidhe—The Fairy Host.

We found no trace of that story in our journeys through

Ulster. Another and more modern influence had overlaid the myth. A man from the Sperrin mountains told us:

I heard that the fairies were the Fallen Angels—ones that was lukewarm, that neither ta'en one side nor the other. When God cast the rebels out of Heaven, the angels that was lukewarm were put out too, and the place that they asked to be sent till was to Ireland—as it was the neartherest place to Heaven. . . .

There are a great number of variants of that story found in Ireland and Scotland and one from the Isle of Barra describes the Fallen Angels 'flying into the holes of the earth just like the stormy petrels'. Below the earthen walls of raths, through fissures of rock, under the gnarled roots of a whitethorn; these are the traditional doors to the fairy world. Where the People of the Sidhe gathered they gave their name to that place. Rashee, the Fort of the Fairies in Antrim; Sheetrim, the Fairy Ridge; Sheean, the Townland of the Fairies in South Armagh; Lisnafeedy, the Fort of Fairy Music. The map of Ulster is haunted with such names.

The Fairy Host it would appear dressed in peasant costume of an antique style: generally in bright colours, red or blue or green. A woman from the Glens of Antrim told of a conversation she had with an old woman in the village of Waterfoot:

Mary, says she, I saw a fairy with my own two eyes.
Augh, says I, you surely didn't see a fairy?
I did—as sure as I have to face my God I saw a fairy. . . . My brother John and I went up for the cows one summer evening and we both saw the wee woman and she wasn't more than two foot high with her wee red cap on her and the wee short skirt, and she walked along the stone ditch and she never moved a pebble o' it!

One well-disposed radio critic, while he enjoyed the series of programmes that resulted from this collection of tales, regretted that 'the experiences never seemed to have happened to the narrator, but to someone else'. Had he been a little more conscientious in his listening he would have heard the farmer from the Mournes who told us:

I seen a fairy myself. We were out on a Sunday evening and up on the ditches—you know what young fellows would be—pulling these haws. Well, I was the smallest—I was only a little tot—and these other bigger fellows was up on this thorn tree just after sunset on a Sunday evening and they were breaking branches with their hands and throwing them down to me. Well, this wee man came at the bottom of the tree and he shouts 'Come down out o' that! Come down out o' that! Come down out o' that!'—and I shouts up, 'Holy Murder—there's a fairy!' And they came down and there was no fairy to be seen. He was gone, and they would make me believe it wasn't so, but I seen the man, a wee man there in a big broad hat on him—that's the God in Heaven's truth—I see it to this day yet!

They were of small stature, two or three feet high. Leprechaun is in Irish luch-corpan, 'mouse-body', and Iubdan, King of the Leprechauns, had in his court a champion reputed to be able to cut down a thistle at one blow. But as W. B. Yeats said: 'Do not think the fairies are always little, everything is capricious about them, even their size. They seem to take what size or shape pleases them.'

The question as to whether the fairies ate food cooked by humans was undecided. We know that their tithe of the harvest was the top pickle of grain, and an Antrim glensman said:

The people that had dealings with the fairies, they never covered the crock of milk nor never counted their scones of bread.

Meal and milk were the two concessions that the invading
Milesians granted to the People of the Sidhe. The country
people still honour them. The story of the borrowed noggin
of meal is so widespread and so frequently offered that I
suspect a recurring stimulus to the idea. We were told several
times of children being mistaken for fairies. An old woman,
asked by a small child for a bowl of meal, might well
through vanity or genuine conviction spread the story that
she had had a visitation. There were, during the bad days
of the Famine and the unemployment among linen workers,
plenty of children sent on this errand. Mr W. F. Marshall,
in his ballad *The Lad*, says of the flax scutchers:

> *Plenishment they'd have little or noan*
> *Except for what they'd stale,*
> *An' they'd make the childher go out an' beg*
> *Gowpins of oaten male.*

In the immemorial give-and-take with the Fairy Host the
country people built round themselves and their household a
bawn of charms and counter-charms against fairy mischief.
And on no occasion was a household more vulnerable than
on the birth of a child.

We heard a hundred stories of stolen children, and almost
as many reasons why they were stolen. The Good People
were paying off an old score; they were envious of the
infant's beauty; the stolen children were taken to the Devil
as ransom; and more pathetically, they were taken in the
hope that they might revive the ancient and dying *sluagh
sidhe*. For the women of the Fairy Race are numerous and
often beautiful, the men few and more often sere and

withered. But whatever the reason there was one give-and-take the countryman feared and was prepared against:

From County Antrim: *They prefer to take boys rather nor girls, and the people to prevent that made all the children wear petticoats and the boys wore them till five or six years of age. I wore them myself—*
From County Down: *Well, every child in the house got oaten meal and salt put on their head in the shape of a cross for fear of the fairies taking them when they went out.*
From County Tyrone: *You weren't to cut the child's nails until it was two-year-old; you were to bite them off with your teeth. You weren't to cut them with scissors for if you cut them with scissors the Gentle People would take it.*

But at times of course to keep the play going the country-folk had to be cheated and defeated, so the fire falls in ash, the nurse nods, and give-and-take is take-and-give. The human infant is spirited away and in its place is left a fairy brat—a changeling. Changelings were the children of their fathers—peevish whining creatures—a bad night's deal for any human infant. But the abducters did not always leave a changeling when they stole a child.

Rosie Mason went one time to see the fairies, said a man from Strangford Lough, *but these young girls were sitting by the roadside and they said, 'Rosie don't go any further—they're there all right.' But Rosie went on for she says, 'I've come too far, seven miles, for not to see them.' So she went on and they were there. She looked in through the windy and she seen that they had taken John Alton's child out of the cradle and they were busy working—cutting a log of wood in the likeness of a child. And the wee captain of the fairies was saying:*

> *Make it stout firm and roon,*
> *Like John Alton's child of Ballyalton Toon;*

Make it stout firm and roon,
Like John Alton's child of Ballyalton Toon. . . .

It was in their efforts to steal newborn children that the
Fairy Host appear most ruthless and malignant. But, no
matter what their age, the country people were never shot
of them. The Good Neighbour was always at their heels
from infancy to old age.

There was a dealer from this part of the Sperrins and he was
away at a fair, and when he was coming home some time in the
night he met a wee funeral of fairies on the road and he grabbed
for a lock of clay and he fired it in the name of the Father, Son
and Holy Ghost on the top of the coffin, and they dropped it,
and he opened it and it was his next door neighbour's woman.
Well, he took her home; his was the next house to hers. When
he got till his own house he put her into the barn and told her to
stay there for a while. So he went in home and his own people
commenced to tell him about such an' a one being dead—terrible
excitement and crying and vexation about the neighbour woman
being dead, and they were running back and forward to the wake.
Well, he listened on and when he got a bite to eat he went over
to the wake and sure enough she was in the bed a-waking; the
likeness of the very same woman.

Well, the house was full of people. He went out as he was the
next door neighbour and carried in a basket of turf and put it on
the fire and fixed it up well and when it was kindling up bravely,
he went out and brought in another basket of turf.

The people at the wake didn't know what he meant—it was far
too hot to have such a fire in the house on a wake. But when it was
right blazing, he reached over to the corpse in the bed and he
lifted it and put it into the fire. The mourners near killed each
other getting out of the door, but all that remained of the corpse
was a black stick on the fire. All was over and the man went back
till his own house and brought back the real woman.

I had an uncle myself, said a man from South Armagh, *and the fairies took him away regular—oh, he came in the latter end to think nothing of it. And my mother's uncle was the same, they took him away four times in the one week. He said he came to know them singly as well as his own neighbours and was never afeared. What call, says he, would I have to be afeared? Divil the button of harm they'd do on me. He said they all wore tall hats—red hats. Many a time, says he, they'd just sit round him on the ditches and laugh at him.*

The fairies hindered or helped; they were whimsical and sullen by turns; malevolent or friendly. They were capricious human beings seen through the wrong end of a telescope. The countryman feared them and bent his wit to safeguard himself, his family and his stock from fairy mischief. He and his wife employed a wide range of periapts; iron, meal and salt, male clothing hung on the cradle, the open tongs and the rowan bush. The rowan was associated with the lightning because of its glowing berries. Thor and the Thunder in general being the sworn enemy of all evil power the rowan was a popular *apotropaeon*.

> *Rowan tree and red thread*
> *Put the fairies to their speed.*

So the countrywoman used the 'fire-tree' to protect her byre and dairy. A woman from the Antrim Glens told us:

I used to see my Aunt Mary putting a rowan spray under the eaves—under the thatch, and it wasn't until long after I learned that it was the custom to protect the cattle.

But in Ulster there are fairies other than those that:

> *Drink dairies dry, and stroke the cattle;*
> *Steal sucklings, and thro' the keyholes sling,*
> *Toping and dancing in a ring.*

Sometimes they would interfere in the everyday work of the farm—for good or bad.

I heard them tell that on a moonlight night they could hear the rattle of the spades as the Gentry were setting a man's praties— oul John McDade was his name—they were busy setting McDade's praties that moonlight night.

A man from Forkhill went out to cut hay one moonlight night and a little wee fellow in a red hat came into the field to him and says 'Mickie, I'll give ye a bit of a hand to cut the hay with a scythe.' 'Very good,' says Mickie, 'start.' The two of them started off and another little wee fellow comes in and he says 'Mickie, I'll give ye a bit of a hand.' 'Very good, very good,' says Mickie, 'start in.' Well, a third one come and a fourth and a fifth and they all started to mow abreast of Mickie. They weren't very long mowing the meadow with six scythes, so Mickie thanked them and went away home. And the next morning he come out and had a look at the meadow and dammit, all that was cut was what he mowed himself. There was only his own cut right through the six cuts.

★

The Fairy Bush or *Skeagh*, whether it stands in ragged company on a forth or in lonely antiquity in the meadow, is, to the countryman, the emblem and epitome of the Fairy Host. When Christianity felled the Five Sacred Trees of Ireland its apostles had only reached the edge of a shadowy forest stretching from the sea to the horizon of mythology. Out of that dark forest came the whitethorn bush. Even to-day only the foolhardy will tamper with it.

That same bush that I'm telling you about, said the Mourne woman,—*my grandfather one day had a big load of corn coming up and the corn catched on this branch, and says my grandfather, 'I'll cut that branch, fairy or no fairy'. And he took a billhook and he cut the branch and the branch fell and his arm fell and he never lifted it to his head till the day he died.*

A *skeagh* that has existed through generations becomes immemorial; it has always been there—its neighbourhood is an 'ould ancient place'. And it contributed to the history of that family—every generation hung a story on its branches.

Well, there is a bush in our field, said the man from South Armagh, *and it's only a very little small bush. About 200 years ago my great-great-grandfather cut it down and when he had it finished—left on the ground—something like water hit him between the eyes. He put up his hand and saw it was blood on his face. He went into the house to get himself cleaned and saw it was blood. When he was in the house a messenger came from Slieve Gullion—he had a horse grazing on it—and the horse had chased down a rock and broke his neck. So he got the bush gathered up again and got help and put a stone on the roots and left it there and it's there from that day to this—and my father wouldn't touch it and he wouldn't let me touch it.*

At set times such as May Eve, lights would hang in the Fairy Thorn; sometimes flying together into a glowing orb, then dancing apart, each separate light inhabited by a little figure beautiful in face and dress. A Gaelic poet has described one of them:

> *Loveliness shone round her like a light*
> *Her steps were music of songs.*

But they were as mischievous as they were beautiful.

My own father, Owen Downey, lived over there, said a woman from the Mournes, *and he was herding at this big bush where they used to see the fairies dancing—over there in my grandfather's place. And it would be all lit up on Halloweve night and on Christmas and on May Eve—it would be all lit up and them dancing, and they would say to my grandfather 'Come on Oweny and have a reel in the field', and they would give him a big red apple, and if he didn't go into the reel it would change to a lump of horse-dung in his hand.*

The little boy's apple that changed in his hand to something useless and unpleasant. The fairy gold with its alloy of malice. And the peasant always dreaming of the treasure that would free him from the landlord and the stony acre.

There was an old woman lived in this townland of Sheean, said a man from Forkhill, *and she had a husband—and her husband and the 'join'* ('join' with a neighbour to complete some work) *was out ploughing in the field one day and she was going round gathering brusheen for to boil the dinner; and she come to a rock and there was a gillycup stuck on the rock and she pulled it off, and when she pulled it off it was full up with gold sovereigns. She took it home and she rolled it up in a cloth and put it in a chest—they used to have chests then—and she went out and she called:*

Hoi, Harry, Harry, come home quick, come home quick! What's wrong?

Come home. We're made up for ever!

He came home as quick as he could—he didn't know what was wrong.

Ah, Harry, she says, we're made up. I found a gillycup and it full of sovereigns!

Come on and get it, get it!

She went to get it and when she took it out and rolled out the rag it was just horse-dung was in it.

Damn your sowl, he says, why didn't ye spit on it? If ye hadda spit on it they couldn't have took it off ye!

The gold was clumsily concealed, but always as the peasant stretched out his hand the treasure vanished.

A man from the Sperrin Mountains said: *One time there was a man at Devan the name of McBride who was ploughing a field on his farm and he came on a crock of goold, and when he saw it he loosed the horses and stuck his plough in by the head to mark where the goold was, and then he pretended to the other man it was dinnertime. He was a greedy man, d'ye see? And he came back alone again to raise the crock of goold. But when he came back there wasn't an inch in the field that hadn't a wooden plough stuck on the crown of its head like his own, so that he was beat out of the crock of goold.*

There was the *oiteagh sluaigh*, 'the fairy whirlblast' that could lift men, women and children and the only way to save them was to hurl your cap or shoe into the wind shouting 'Mine is yours and yours is mine!' whereupon the abducted person was dropped back to earth. Strangely enough, this form of locomotion was rarely if ever used for the transportation of human midwives so necessary at fairy births, but was usually the beginning to some mischievous prank as in the adventure of John McCrory from the Sperrin Mountains:

A man named McCrory who lived in Croft one night went out and stood at the gable of the house to look at the night, and a blast of wind came and lit him in England and he was in England two years, as he thought. So he earned a lot of money and at the end of the two years thought about coming home, so he arrived back at his house at about nine o'clock one night. When he came in, the wife was sitting spinning, just as when he left, and the daughter was baking bread at the table, so he said 'it's a strange thing you were spinning when I left, and you were baking bread, and I'm away two years and you never spoke to me or welcomed me back again'. And the wife laughed and said, 'away two years— you're away about two minutes!' 'I'm away two years and I have the proof. There's a new dress I've brought for Biddy'—that was the daughter—'and there's a shawl for you'. He went over and opened the parcel with the dress and when he opened it, it was a parcel of horse-dung; and he said 'I'll open the shawl for you, Susan', and when he opened it, the same material was in that parcel. So he said 'well, I'll show you the real proof' and he put his hand in his pocket to pull out all the money he had, and when he pulled out the money it was a fistful of horse-dung.

That was the fairy treasure. The gold was always found in a croak of laughter. The old people never flitted away from the stony mountainside and the Good Neighbour. That is why we were able to find them.

Chapter Six

TRAVELLING TO THE FAIR

On the strangford lough road that runs from Killyleagh to Comber lies the village of Ardmillan. As a village it's no great shakes, but picturesque enough with tumbled whitewashed walls, ruffled thatch and climbing roses, the blooms buttoned and bunched together. The inhabitants, like those of any inland village, work in the fields and neighbouring towns, for as a means of livelihood the lough means very little to them. This wasn't always so. At one time Ardmillan was a fishing village and launched a fleet in pursuit of the lough herring. In those days, a century and more ago, the women of the village were as skilful as the men in handling boats, particularly the four-oar racing gigs. They still tell stories in the district of one famous crew, Jean Gilmore and the three sisters, Betty, Jean and Amy Long. For years this crew and their craft were unbeaten in the gig-races in Larne, Belfast and Strangford Loughs. After a race at an Antrim port a crew of local men, exasperated at being beaten for the second successive year by the Ardmillan women, seized the prize-money. Although the sex of the victors must have been evident to any unbiassed spectator, the defeated crew were indelicate enough to suggest an investigation. To the excited hurroos of the crowd the four fair rowers strode forward as one woman on their inquisitors; the men parted with the money without as much as another cheep.

Perhaps the feeding grounds in the lough became exhausted or it may have been one of those inexplicable migrations of the herring that finished the Ardmillan fleet. But while the hauls lasted the fishermen of Ardmillan had their moments. One evening when they were on the lough a storm blew up and drove them across three or four miles of water to the village of Kircubbin on the other side. The Kircubbin people with their usual hospitality found beds and shelter for the men until the storm died. The following day a number of Kircubbin and Ardmillan men went to the local pub for a parting cup or two. At last an Ardmillan man was permitted to buy a round. As he dropped the change into his purse he said: 'D'ye know, boys, things are as cheap here as they are in Ireland!'

No one is under an obligation to believe this story, though it might very well be true. Not, I may add, because the man from Ardmillan was likely to know less about the outside world than another, but because of the *immobility* of the countryman even as recently as thirty or forty years ago. He travelled to church or chapel, to the scutch-mill, the smiddy or the cobbler; in the evening, if he was the sociable type, he took the field pad to his neighbour's hearth. All these lay within his own townland. The great occasions, the occasions in which he saw beyond his own drumlins, were when he travelled to the market or the fair.

Not everyone could afford to go to market. If a man took his wife she was expected to look after the sale of butter and eggs while he attended to other business. There was no room in the country cart for old people or jaunting children. Every strong farmer considered it his duty to inform those neighbours who were too old to travel, or did not own a horse, of his intended visit to the town, and on the evening before market they would bring him their errands. There were grave deliberations between the men of the house as to what was needed for the outdoor life of the farm, and the women presented their list of requirements: poultry rings, thread, American cloth, condiments, dried fruit, rennet and the other simple luxuries of the farm kitchen.

I remember as a child sitting on the fringe of a group of men one evening at Ballymacashon cross-roads. Behind us, fifteen miles away, the sky was silvered over Belfast. It was a Friday night and the men were discussing among a host of other topics that day's market prices in the city. A youth of about sixteen years of age had been there for the first time in his life, and the story of his day still flowed from him.

His friend, a lad of the same age, eyed him wistfully.
'Charlie,' he whispered, 'whit like are the trams?' The bats
hunted the hedgerows for moths as Charlie scratched his
downy chin and hunted for a simile. 'I'll tell ye whit,' he
said at last, 'they're like twa lang-cars cowped yin on tap o'
ither, baith painted rid, and the hale yoke rins on iron
trecks.'

The reference to long-cars dates that cross-roads gathering.
It was in fact about 1922, when the first motor-buses were
bouncing along the metalled roads sending dust and
pedestrians to the tops of the sheughs.

It is difficult for us to realise how much the introduction
of the bus revolutionised the set ways of country life. Until
its arrival the women of the farm were accustomed to walk
long distances to market their butter and eggs. It must be
said, however, that it was often in search of a better price
rather than lack of transport that drove them on these
weary journeys. The women of the Bailieboro' district in
County Cavan were known to walk the twelve miles to
Cootehill or Kells because they could get a penny a pound
more for their butter at these markets than they could at
Bailieboro' market. Whether the utopian fares charged
by the owners of the early 'private' buses would have made
the twelve mile run along the Cavan roads worth while, I
cannot say, but I know that in those parts of County Down
remote from railway stations the market day bus ride became
a social event.

All this of course meant little to the men of the house, who
still had to drive their cattle or pigs along the dark morning
roads to the fair. Their only hope of a shortened journey was

to meet a dealer on the road outside the town and strike a bargain with him. The briskness of trade was judged by the number of buyers and 'tanglers' who left the fair and came out along the roads to bargain with the incoming cattle-owners. But the appearance of dealers on the road could apparently be a misleading phenomenon, and many a man who drove his cattle past them ended the day by losing money on the fair-hill.

As to which is the greater philanthropist, the dealer or the farmer with stock to sell, I should be loath to decide. But I can heartily commend a cattle deal to a young actor who wishes to extend his range of mime and expression: for there he can observe, more rapidly than I can write them down, stunned awe, amused tolerance, inexhaustible patience, simulated deafness, magnanimity, inarticulate fury, moving appeals to Providence and a frightening rigor of hands buried in pockets or hidden under coat tails.

'The bargain-striker and the "tangler",' it has been said, 'are the only men who go to a cattle fair without cattle and come away from it with money in their pockets.' The 'tanglers' bought beasts from the farmers and 'tangled' them, that is, immediately put them up for sale at the same fair in the hope of making a profit. The activities of the bargain-striker, or 'split-the-differs' as he was called in some districts, are much better known. His self-imposed task was to drag out the reluctant hands and strike them together in a bargain. If he could coax a decent 'luck-penny' from the seller, the buyer usually gave him some share of it. The least he could expect, if he was a drinking man, was a glass in the nearest pub, when the money had finally been paid over at the steps of the Town Hall, or wherever, in that particular fair, was the customary place of settlement.

The bargain-striker had to be a man of infinite patience and good-humour, for until such times as they've settled down to the serious business of bargaining, he was the butt of both buyer and seller. I remember watching a 'split-the-differs' trail a dealer through Moy Fair. Time after time he tried to bring the prospective buyer back to where the farmer with his patient beasts stood under the trees. (Though it must be said that the dealer didn't wander too far away, for by doing so he would have immediately relinquished his position to another prospective buyer. He moved about just within earshot examining tractor-appliances, buckets, horses, sheep, and registering amusement, indifference, even downright disgust every time his eye chanced to rest on the cattle he intended to buy.)

'Split-the-differs' hailed him once again: 'Come on, now, come on, now, we're wasting this good man's time—'

Dealer: 'His time's his own. If ye can get a better customer nor me, don't be wasting *your* time—'

Split-the-differs: 'Ah, come now. You were tellin' me the s'morning what ye were looking in the fair. Now, look at them animals—don't they just fit the bill? Tell me that now, don't they just fit the bill? And for the handful of shillin's that's between ye—'

Dealer: 'Handful of shillin's, how-are-ye! You're a dangerous boyo, Mulvee, ye would talk me into anything—'

Split-the-differs: 'Aye, God help ye, it's a wonder they

let you out alone! Come on, now, ye wouldn't break my word with the dacent man—'

Dealer: 'Oh, b'God I would! I hae broken my own before this!'

Split-the-differs: 'Now you haven't that reputation—'

And so it goes on until at last buyer and seller are brought together in a splutter of flattery and denigration, hand is slapped in hand and split-the-differs gets his reward.

As to the origin of the bargain-striker, it was an Antrim glensman who assured me that it could be traced to the early eighteenth-century fairs where roving cattle-drovers acted as interpreters between the Irish-speaking peasants and the English-speaking planters. I mentioned this to a folklorist but he didn't show any great enthusiasm for the theory, nor would he agree that the ancient fair held at Orriter in County Tyrone, and known as *Aonach-na-gealta*, could, with any accuracy, be translated as the Fair of the Strangers or Protestants. 'For one thing,' he added enigmatically, 'the *aontaighe* were places of merrymaking.'

Most Ulster people have heard the heart-cry of the deluded farmer:

> *'Twas the daling-men*
> *From Crossmaglen*
> *Put whiskey in my tae!*

If it is likely that I have misquoted the lines it is just as probable that they have no foundation in fact. But it must be conceded that when it comes to stories of sellers in the hands of unscrupulous dealers, a voluminous anthology, from credulous Moses and his gross of green spectacles to the pub-chatter at any present-day fair, could be gathered with little trouble. It would be more difficult to mount a counter-blast, for dealers, understandably enough, are reluctant to admit the possibility of being diddled. The problem is to combine an unshakeable integrity with the cunning of the expert. As a dealer once told me: 'If you're too damn smart in a bargain, even if it's only luck, it might take you years to live it down with that man *and all his connection.* Ah, now,' he continued, 'it's an old saying in the cattle trade that a dealing-man usually dies with a light blanket over him.'

'I'd like to believe that.'

'It's true enough. You can have a good year or a bad year —Luck's a King or Luck's a Beggar. A dealing-man can't foretell from day to day what his chance will bring. I remember one old cow-dealer telling another that he was going to quit the business. "There's no profit in it," says he. "Ah," said the other, "there's a high reward for ye. Is there not a place called Purgatory in your Church?" "There is," said the first. "Well, you'll get your reward in Heaven. You've had your Purgatory already with bad cows on this earth. What more profit d'ye want?" '

And in the days before cattle-grading was introduced, 'bad cows' at the fair were not uncommon. There was the peculiar complaint called 'bunker' and the beast affected by it developed a lower lip not unlike that of a pig. 'That beast,' said a dealer, 'might be in perfect condition every day of the week, but if you killed it you might as well eat cord—its meat would be all strings. So the dealer always looked at the lips. Some cattle have what is called "a pig's mouth", the lower jaw is shorter than the upper one. You would know by the lips that the beast was a "bunker"—it wouldn't thrive—it couldn't eat enough good grass because of the shape of its mouth.'

I can't pretend to any great knowledge of livestock faults and blemishes, or the tricks used at fairs to conceal them. Horses in particular seemed to have been the victims of ingenious and cruel doctoring to make them appear sound. The 'gingering' of tired old nags to make them appear mettlesome is notorious. Recently I heard of a trick, which if it wasn't an effort to conceal a blemish was undoubtedly an attempt to deceive a prospective buyer. Years ago, dealers from the North of England attended the Irish fairs to buy two-year-old cattle, which naturally cast two front teeth at that age. So the farmers to oblige the North country-men took a hammer and a harrow-pin and knocked the two front teeth out of their year-and-a-half cattle.

The fairs of course weren't given over entirely to the buying and selling of cattle. On that day the windswept streets and the staring squares of the town would fill up with honest folk pursuing honest occupations and rascals pursuing occupations that lacked antecedents and indentures. There were the 'stocking women' who stood in the entrances to the tavern yards and knitted feet into the stockings of the 'men without weemin at home'. They charged from 4d to 6d a pair. There were quacks and Indian doctors such as the noted Dr Sequah who was a famous figure at the Ulster fairs fifty or sixty years ago. 'He would arrive in the fair with a six piece brass band. His carriage was drawn up

in the market-square and people who were suffering from
stiffness in the joints were oxtered up into the carriage in
turn. The Doctor with three or four assistants then started
rubbing some rare ointment into the patient's limbs. They
would rub it in with their bare knuckles until the patient
would be roaring and shouting with the pain, but the band
kept blattering away all the time and not a haet of his
hullabaloo would you hear! When the patient got out he
was as soople as a sally-rod—all his aches and stiffness gone—
and he'd throw away his stick and walk without it. But
in a wheen of days he was as bad as ever, for he and his
household could never apply the rare ointment the way
Dr Sequah and his helpers could.'

In the canvas town that arose overnight in the market
place were the stalls and sideshows of the rope and harness
sellers, the 'cheeny-man' who could beat the most fragile
of plates together without chipping them, the vendors of
soaps and candles, the man who permitted himself to be
tied up and then with a shake and a wriggle shrugged off
his ropes (he used a chain, I am told, in the villages around
Lough Neagh where the Lough fishermen had left him
trussed so tightly that the police had to cut him free on
several occasions). There was the hawker with his fresh
herrings, the seller of sweetmeats, the ballad-singer with
his fresh words to an old tune, for in Ireland a new ballad
flies to a melody like a woman to a mirror. There was the
dealer in second-hand clothes with his traditional spiel:
'Who'll give me £2 for this coat? Neither crack nor brack,
flaw nor ravel. All right, who'll give me thirty-five bob?
Perfect in every shape and form. Ye could wear it to High

Mass, Low Mass, or no Mass at all. Ah well, who'll give me thirty bob for it? Whoever likes can try it on. This coat, let me inform ye, was specially made for a high-ranking officer in the army who had to go on foreign service before the tailor had it finished. The tailor got more for making it than thirty shillings. Never mind—if ye haven't got thirty shillings I'll take twenty-five. Look at the tweed in it —it would stretch a yard before it would tear an inch and wear like a woman's tongue. Will anybody give twenty-five bob for it? Maybe its charity ye want. I'll give it to ye. Give me a pound for the sake of charity and take the coat. Poor St Patrick, the Patron Saint of Ireland—he was right. He passed through this town and said it might prosper but he doubted it. . . .'

★

'I've seen them coming down that hill,' said the old man pointing along the street that led to Rathfriland, 'agh, just wee cuts of school children some of them, and when they got into Newry here, the eating-houses would have baps and cups of tea ye could swim a duck in, set out on forms. That cost them three-ha'pence. Did ye ever eat a bap? My ould granny used to call them "pastry". She had a wee rhyme—

> *Boys-a-boys I found a penny*
> *Boys-a-boys I bought a bap*
> *Boys-a-boys I ate it up*
> *Boys-a-boys it made me fat—*

—though there was never much fat on her in my day. There was some bliddy ruffians that kept eating-houses here in them days. They would set out big three-legged pots of soup on the pavements and sell it till the boys and girls that came in for the hiring. D'ye know what was in it? It was nothing but hot water with a handful or two of boiled cabbage thrown in, and they would give it a rummle round with a talla candle to put grease rings on the top of it, like it was real broth made with bones. That was bad enough at the May Fair, but in November the wind off them mountains would freeze the balls off a pawnbroker's sign. That was the fairs they hired at, May and November, surely.'

May and November surely, the thresholds in the countryman's year that circles below the prosaic calendar. Not only were the hiring fairs held in these months but in some districts the 'gale-days' in which rents were paid were so arranged as to coincide with the fairs. 'Crooked Willie', a land-agent whose name is still malodorous in a district in Tyrone, lifted his rents at a certain fair in that county. He had, apparently, a liking for sovereigns and half-sovereigns, and no matter in what coinage a tenant offered his rent, 'Crooked Willie' insisted on the bulk of it being paid in gold. The only place where the cottiers were likely to find this class of money was in the largest shop in the village, which, by happy chance, was run by 'Crooked Willie's' sister. The lady, to compensate herself for the extra labour, added a small service charge of a shilling on a sovereign. When she ran out of gold piece 'Crooked Willie's' collection was huddled back across the street to her for 'resale' to the cottiers. This profitable game came to an end some years later when 'Crooked Willie' was discovered, one winter's morning, submerged in a bog-hole into which, presumably, he had wandered.

The presence of so many young people at the hiring fairs gave them an atmosphere of gaiety and vivacity. There were, of course, other fairs where traditionally 'the young ones sported themselves'. 'At the Lammas Fair at Gortin,' said a Sperrin man, 'you be to take your girl out if you had one, and walk her up and down the street, and take her in for a treat. I don't know why, only it was a rule. You'd walk up and down the whole day. The girls would be specially dressed surely. They'd try to have a new coat and hat and shoes. And the boy would wear the best he had. That was a very special day, a day mentioned in early times.'

And the fairs of seedtime and harvest as well as those of 'the feast of first-fruits' were mentioned in early times. But unlike the Lammas fairs, the gaiety at the hiring fairs marked the few hours of liberty between leaving the service of one master and hiring with the next. The young people came into the fair each with his or her bundle, 'for no master would take on a servant who didn't have another shirt and a pairs of boots'. A Newtownhamilton man told me that the farmers felt the arms and shoulders of the boys and girls, though I've heard this just as emphatically denied in other districts. But 'a good stance and a hard palm' were considered essential. If the master and the man came to an agreement the master paid over an 'erle' ranging, in different fairs, from a shilling to a half-crown. This, traditionally, was spent in the pubs or eating-houses before the new servant left the fair. The 'erle' was supposed to bind the servant to his new employer, and servants who in their enthusiasm for employment went round the fair collecting numerous 'erles' were often prosecuted.

The length of service usually ran from May to November and again from November to May, but there were also Quarter Day fairs where labourers and servants hired themselves for terms from the 1st of February to the May fair and from Lammas to the November fair. Other variations in the terms of service were those of the man who worked 'half-time' for two neighbouring farmers and the difference acknowledged between the 'hired' and the 'bound'; the hired man slept at his master's farm and the bound man slept at home. The following three statements noted in different parts of the Province give a fair idea of the changes that have taken place in the payment of hired servants in the past hundred years.

'At the time of the Famine in 1846-7, my grandfather, a strong able-bodied man, was working for 8*d* a day without diet. My grandmother was wheeling stones for 2*d* a day and she had to support herself. In bad districts I heard of men working for 3*d* a day, and in some cases when digging potatoes they had to go to work so early in the morning that they brought a lamp to set on the ridge and show them what they were doing.' (Co. Armagh.)

'Before the First World War a first-class ploughman—a man who was able to do all the horse-work of a farm—was given a free house and small garden and a wage of from 9/- to 12/- a week. He had to support himself, but in some cases got his dinner. A first-class servant man got from £9 to £11 for a half-year. Boys got from £5 to £7 and fully-grown girls from £4 to £5.' (Co. Tyrone.)

'The last hiring fair I mind was in Castlewellan in 1933 and they were offering good-class ploughmen up to £40 and their keep for the half-year.' (Co. Down.)

For a description of the conditions under which the hired servant worked I refer you to the ballad-sellers. The stories differ: of sleeping in lofts and feeding in outhouses; of a boy or a girl 'who had neither in them nor on them' taken into the farmer's family and enjoying for the first time solid food and warm clothing. I'll compromise with the County Armagh ballad-maker's lament:

> I went up into the market to a place
> they call the stand,
> And for six long months I hired with
> a man called Tom McCann.
> I arrived all right next morning
> as plainly you will see.
> He gave me eggs and bacon and then
> shook hands with me.
> Saying, Johnnie you are welcome,
> you are welcome to the land;
> But little I knew what I'd to do for
> Mr Tom McCann.
>
> That night as I lay on my bed
> in agony did roll
> The fleas they made a strong attack
> my kidneys for to hold.
> I shouted holy murder, but they
> still kept clinging on
> Oh what a terrible time I had with
> that man called Tom McCann.

He called me down to breakfast,
no breakfast could I see.
Only six big hungry children crying
'is there anything left for me'.
The butter that was on the bread no
human eye could scan.
For tea you need not mention it with
Mr Tom McCann.

The weather bein' wet and stormy
it bein' in the winter time.
I'd roads to make and drains to clean
to mix and scatter lime.
You must be a good servant and do the
best you can;
Or I greatly fear you won't be here!
cried Mr Tom McCann.

The skin grew tight upon me,
my hair grew like a wig.
My trousers got too wide for me,
my coat got far too big.
I prayed to God that He might send
a coffin or a van
To take me from that vagabond called
Mr Tom McCann.

A host of small customs and traditions and beliefs have
eluded this chapter on Fairs. Some of them are as long dead
and departed as the Irish razor-back pig. Others are withering
daily under the breath of Government Marketing Boards.
To-day, in some parts of Ulster, men and women still twine
red thread into the tails of their cattle before they drive

them to market. It is a periapt. They would be politely surprised at your surprise. They could show you the stretch of road where the cattle might be 'blinked'. To protect their animals is the sensible and commonplace thing to do. 'Custom,' said Stephen Dedalus, 'is a mark of ordinariness.'

Chapter Seven

DANCING AT THE FEIS

A DISTINGUISHED EUROPEAN FOLKLORIST, a fellow Ulsterman of mine, once remarked to me that if Saint Patrick were to return to Ireland he would most probably be discovered at some hearth listening to the tales of Pagan Ireland. The paradox amused me although the thought did pass through my mind that the saint who will sit in judgment on all Irishmen at the Final Trump might also be politely interested in the fortunes of this island since

A.D. 461: then, advisedly, perhaps not. The limits of saintly patience are proverbial.

But it wasn't until I came on a copy of *Silva Gadelica* and read therein the Colloquy of the Ancients that I appreciated my friend's half-earnest remark. In this narrative Patrick meets Caeilte, one of the surviving heroes of the shattered Fianna, and listens attentively to the old warrior's stories:

When Caeilte had told Patrick of the drinking horns that were in Finn's house, Patrick said: 'Victory and blessing wait on thee Caeilte! For the future thy stories and thyself are dear to us; and now tell us another tale.'

'I will indeed; but say what story thou woulds't be pleased to have?'

'In the Fianna had ye horses or cavalry?'

Caeilte answered: 'We had so; thrice fifty foals from one mare and a single sire.'

'Whence were they procured?'

'I will tell thee the truth of the matter. . . .'

'All this,' said Patrick, 'is to us a recreation of spirit and of mind, were it not only a destruction of devotion and a dereliction of prayer.'

. . . and Patrick's two guardian angels came to him, of whom he enquired whether in God's sight it were convenient for him to be listening to the stories of the Fianna. With equal emphasis, and concordantly, the angels answered him:

'Holy cleric, no more than a third part of their stories do these ancient warriors tell, by reason of forgetfulness and lack of memory; but by thee be it written on tabular staffs

of poets, and in ollaves' words; for to the companies and
nobles of the latter time to give ear to these stories will be
for a pastime!' Which said, the angels departed.

By the sixth century the tolerance of the sea-faring
Patrick and the native affection of princely Columcille for
the poets, minstrels and story-tellers seems to have evapo-
rated from the councils of the ecclesiastics. The last Feis of
Tara assembled under the presidency of Dermot MacFergus,
the Ard Righ, in the year 560, was cursed and proscribed
by St Ruadhan of Lorrha as a rallying place of the Prince of
Darkness. This saint, under a variety of pseudonyms,
is still active on many of our rural councils.

Thirteen and a half centuries later the Gaelic League
reintroduced the Feis to 'encourage and revive interest in
Irish music, Irish dancing and the Irish language'. The
first Feis under the new dispensation was held in Belfast in
1900. It was enthusiastically supported by Protestants as
well as Roman Catholics for this fresh flowering of Irish
culture coincided with the bright autumnal leaves of Irish
Liberalism. The great political upheavals in the following
years destroyed this concord, and the process was hastened
by the obtuse insistence on the part of the organisers to
carry over the festivals from Saturdays into Sundays;
this innovation was no less repugnant to Protestants fifty
years ago than it would be to-day.

But of course all the competitors at a country feis do not
belong to one section of the community. In Ireland, the
musician or the story-teller, regardless of where he worships,
is welcome wherever he goes. One of the finest traditional
fiddlers in Ulster, a Presbyterian, has played at practically

every feis in the Province. Although he has now laid up his fiddle and bow (except for the odd ceilidhe among his neighbours) his protégés still appear on feis platforms as far apart as Castleblaney in County Monaghan and Cushendall in the Glens of Antrim.

Some years ago I travelled with a friend to *Feis na nGleann*, held that year in the vale of Glenariff. There are larger and more elaborate gatherings in the calendar of Feiseanna than the Feis of the Glens, but none can offer a more seemly background to the musicians, dancers and athletes than the mountains of Lurigedan and Carn-neill that frame the Glen of the Arrif.

The hotels and boarding-houses of Cushendall, Cushendun and Waterfoot were booked out. In the village of Waterfoot I saw a party of kilted Scots who had crossed the ancient seaway from Kintyre to Antrim. The number-plates of the cars lining the village streets indicated that visitors from a dozen counties had travelled north and east for the feis. The village streets, the pubs, the hotel lounges, sounded to hail and farewell in Irish.

Sharing our luncheon table in the hotel were two bright-faced lads, scarcely out of their teens, with the *fianne* of the Gaelic speaker in the lapels of their jackets. As they chatted across the table I nudged my friend: 'Are you eaves-dropping?'

'Yes.'

'What are they saying?'

He carefully swallowed a mouthful of salmon: 'They are discussing the pens of their respective aunts.'

The little waitress brought the dessert. She was sturdy,

round-faced, auburn-haired, energetic. One of the lads
spoke to her in Irish, a phrase, nothing more. Her face lit
up. She laid down the plates and answered him at length
with gesture, pout, shake of the head, frown, smile. I could
see my companion, in sympathy, nod, smile, frown. God
knows what raillery and gay badinage I was missing.
Sneakingly I mimicked the nods and smiles, and out of the
corner of my eye I could see the young fellows doing
likewise. At last the little waitress shook out her final
cascade of words like twinkling fish from a net and hurried
away.

'And what was all that about?' I asked.

'She's a wee girl from Donegal,' answered my companion. He folded his napkin methodically, a reminiscent
smile on his lips.

'Bah!' I said, 'you can tell me about it after lunch.'

I glanced at the young fellow across the table. His neck
was a healthy pink and although I didn't like to stare I got
the impression somehow that his *fianne* had become a little
lack lustre.

★

A different district in the Antrim Glens is selected each
year in which to stage *Feis na nGleann*. This year it was
divided between Cushendall and Glenariff, 'the Queen of
the Nine Glens' which is about two miles southward along
the coast from Cushendall. When we arrived there was a big
marquee set up in a field in the floor of the glen; a flutter of
little flags marked the running track and in the corner of
the field two raised platforms had been set up for the

dancers. In the sports field there was that active bustling ordered disorder that one always associates with an athletic meeting, when two or three events are in progress at the same time.

The hammer is thrown by athletes with centuries of tradition in this sport behind them; the javelin rises in a high glittering arc against the dark mountain. And through all the chatter and laughter and shouts of the great crowd who have gathered here to-day, the ubiquitous fiddler insinuates himself. There he sits high on the platform, one knee cocked on the other unreeling a ribbon of music for the dancers. He was playing a reel that I knew, 'The Maids of Tulla'.

'Who were the Maids of Tulla?' I asked my friend.

'I only know it as an air and I advise you not to go chasing relevance through the titles of Irish dance music. What, for example, do you hope to make of Upstairs in a Tent or The Piper's Picnic or Saft Tam's Hornpipe or Fasten the Leggin'?'

'Well, Saft Tam . . .'

'Have you ever met him?'

'Let me think . . .'

'You haven't and you never will. He's a figment of a frenzied fiddler's imagination. I'll tell you something. Here in County Antrim they have a pleasant custom called the Fiddlers' Meeting. Anything up to twelve or fourteen traditional fiddlers meet at a farmhouse and play away at each other all night until both elbows ache.'

'Both?'

'Both, surely. Obviously a certain amount of refreshment

is called for. A fiddler takes the floor. Suddenly his bow
trots away in a quite unpremeditated run of melody.

' "That's a new one!" somebody shouts.

'He plays it again assisted by the memory of his fellow-
musicians. There's no doubt about it; it's a new one.

' "What'll ye call it?" That's the question.

'Now, country fiddlers are as notorious for their modesty
as they are for their geniality. The innovator's eye ranges
round the company. He sees the farmhand grinning at him
out of the lamp's shadows. "B'God!" he shouts, "I'll call
it—"

'Saft Tam's Hornpipe?'

'Exactly.'

'And do you really believe that tunes and titles are arrived
at quite so fortuitously as that?'

'Well, titles—yes; I'm not so sure about tunes. D'you
know Sean O'Boyle the folk-song collector?'

'I know Sean well.'

'Some time ago I heard him say in a discussion about Irish
music that we had clung to the scales that Europe discarded
in the seventeenth century, but collectors have doctored
and transmogrified our loveliest songs to make jigs and
reels and hornpipes; we have lost or mislaid the words
that first informed many of the most beautiful of our
melodies. If what he says is right, and O'Boyle is not a man
to pass the light word when it comes to Irish music, then the
sooner we start spending a few quid on the *discovery* of
music in the Province the better. But here,' said my friend,
'are the dancers I came to see.'

As we talked the competitors in the vivid costumes had

been mounting the platform, dancing and then retiring to
give way to other teams. Saffron costumes replaced blue,
blue replaced purple as the sets followed each other. As the
dancers poised with pointed toe waiting to move into the
pattern of the jig or reel their embroidered hoods fluttered
in the little wind that blew down from the hills. To say that
the dancers moved into the pattern of the dance is no trite
figure of speech. I am told that the intricacy of the Irish
figure dances closely resembles the interlaced designs in
ancient Irish missals and that the onlooker should be able
to trace a Celtic design in the movements of these dances.
I must say that this refinement escaped me, but my knowledge of Celtic design is limited to gaping through jewellers'
plate-glass at the outsides of those massy silver coffers
with which the citizens of Belfast rejoice visiting notabilities.

The dress of the Irish dancer, pretty as it may be, is of
doubtful antiquity, its like was never seen in *Tir na nOg* or
Tandragee. One historian has gone so far as to say that the
boys and girls should wear Irish peasant garb. What that
is or where he hopes to find the pattern I do not know;
certainly not in the Young Farmers' Clubs. If it means copy-
ing from eighteenth-century prints, better let the hare sit,
for the contemporary costume is attractive and no doubt
admirably suited to the purpose of the dance. And we can
comfort ourselves with the reflection that in Ireland, north
and south, what was a sentimental innovation yesterday,
can, by a bit of astute and unanimous support from the
right quarters, become an ancient and unquestionable
tradition by to-morrow.

My friend was watching a set from Belfast, four girls and

two boys. They were dancing the Harvest Time Jig, a progressive dance in which the dancers face each other in lines of three, a man between two women. As they danced he told me the story of the Harvest Time Jig: it is said to have originated on the West Coast of Ireland during the harvest season when most of the men had gone off to the horrors of tattie-howking in Scotland and England. The dance is so designed that each man has two women partners. As I watched the faces of the dancers, teemed of all expression, and their adroit and flickering feet I could almost subscribe to the hypocrisy that out of poverty and degradation cometh forth beauty.

Feis na nGleann is finished for another year. The sun has drawn away to the head of the glen and the mountain cheeks that seemed so smooth in the heat of the day are suddenly wrinkled with shadows. The dancing platforms are bare and the crowds are massing round the big field for the final event in the programme, the hurling match between Ballycastle and Lochguile. We drift with them like tea-leaves drawn to the side of a cup.

As we balanced our elbows on the swinging top wire of the fence and proceeded to take in the run of the game, a Lochguile player caught the dropping puck on the blade of his caman, and steadied it as it hung in mid-air; there was a flash of his blade, a crack, and the puck went flying up the field again. 'Oh, very nice!' said my friend.

'Fairish to fair,' said the man leaning on the wire beyond him. He was an elderly man, big in the body, dressed in a port-wine brown suit. He had arched his body so that a watch-chain, made from some yellow metal, wouldn't catch on the wire. His crisp new hat was pushed back on his head and there was a red rim round his brow. The game was now a skirmish at the other end of the pitch. Our interest was only engaged slightly, our partisan sympathies not at all.

'You didn't think much of that stroke?' enquired my friend politely.

'He hit it a blarge and trusted to God to do the rest,' said the man. A note in his voice attracted my attention, an English inflexion that even his choice of idiom couldn't conceal.

'And that's not enough?'

'Not half enough, nor quarter enough.'

I leaned across. 'You've played this game yourself, of course?'

'I was one of the first to play it in the Glens.' I listened attentively. There was no doubt about it, the man was an Englishman.

He turned, and for the first time gave us his attention. 'I won the high jump, the half-mile and the hammer-throwing at this feis forty years ago,' he said.

'So?' said my friend, and for the next ten minutes we followed the game with the closest interest.

He took up the thread again. 'Of course, hurling's a very new sport in this district,' he said.

We smiled.

'When we were lads we used to play "shinny", a game not unlike the Scottish shinty.' (That 'Scottish' gave him away badly.)

'And how long have they played hurling here?'

'Oh, not above fifty or sixty years. I played both, of course—'

'Of course,' we echoed.

It was half-time. A small boy came through the crowd with a basket of soft drinks. 'Will you have one?' my friend asked. The big man stared at him in silence and he let the third bottle slip back into the basket.

'It was a grand game, shinny, and it's a pity it was ever let die out. We played it thirteen a side. Only goals counted, no points—like in hurling—only goals. We had a grand way of deciding choice of ends,' and he opened his large hand and smiled reminiscently. 'We never tossed a coin—'

'Is that so?'

'No, what we did was this. The captain of one side tossed his shinny stick to the captain of the other side who caught the hold of it in his right hand. Then the first fella gripped above the other's hold—like this, d'you see? and the second man above *his* hold and turn about until only one handsbreadth was left. The man who had the last grip got the choice of ends. That's how it was done.'

The game was being fought out in the dusk at the other end of the pitch and the big man suddenly tired of it. 'To hell with this,' he said straightening up. We looked at him, he must have been about six feet four. 'If you're walking down the village to the ceilidhe we could stop on the way for a *drink*. That is, of course, if you take a *drink*.'

We followed him out of the field and down the road to the village. We had our drink and then we went along to the parochial hall where the ceilidhe was being held. There we met a mutual acquaintance, a fiddler in the band. As yet there was only a handful of people in the hall and the band was seated on four chairs smoking and ignoring pleas to 'strike up, Ownie boy!'

'D'you see that big man in the brown suit at the door, there?' said I to the fiddler. 'He tells us he won the hammer, the half-mile and the high jump forty years ago . . .'

The fiddler smiled. 'Did he tell ye he was the stroke of the best four-oar gig on this coast forty year ago?'

'No, really?' and we both laughed.

Our fiddler friend didn't. 'Well, he should have, for he was. He was the best bloody natural athlete that ever came out of Antrim. Then when he was a young lad he had to go to sea—there was about sixteen in the family. After that he joined the Liverpool Dock Police and married an Englishwoman—a fine girl. They never missed spending their holidays here every year. And after she died he still come over—every year. What d'ye think o' that?'

'And that bit about the shinny?'

The fiddler winked. 'He's your man,' he said.

I walked to the door and stood beside the big man. 'That's a fine evening,' I said. He looked down at me. 'Ah, the Belfast fella. It is: it's a grand evening. A *grand* evening.'

We stepped outside to let half a dozen lads and girls enter the hall. I stood beside him watching the tumult of colour above the mountains. In the glen two or three boys were drawing the flags from the running-track and the smell of crushed grass hung in the air.

'Tell me,' said the big man, 'did you ever hear of Raftery the Poet?'

'I did.'

'He wrote a thing,' he threw back his head, '. . . *if I could but stand in the heart of my people, old age would drop from me and youth would come back.*'

He pointed a thumb in the direction of the gold chain across his waistcoat. 'That's me,' he said.

In the hall the drummer struck his sound-box three times.

Chapter Eight

GIVE US A BAR

IF AN ULSTER COUNTRYMAN asks you to write out a song for him don't start worrying about your proficiency in tonic sol-fa or staff notation. He'll be wanting the words only. The air he can pick up at home if he doesn't know it already. His ear is his guide for the tune but his heart is in the words. He likes a song with a story in it, or perhaps I should say that he looks on singing as the adornment of a good story. That's why he sees no crying need for a song to have instrumental accompaniment and why he prefers a good song at the kitchen fire to ten at the piano in the parlour.

The songs that please him are those that have grown out of his own environment, the field, the fair, the pages of history. They tell of the rollicking fun of weddings and wakes, hangings and shipwrecks, the heartlessness of landlords and the sorrows of the emigrant ship. And everywhere you go you'll hear people singing the praises of their native place whether it's Magheralin or Magherally, for there (and there alone) there's honey on the docken leaves.

Some years ago I was working in the remote and lovely countryside of the Derg valley that lies between the village of Killeter and the Donegal border. In this district you're treading closer to the hem of bygone time than probably in any other district of Ulster. I was shown the remains of a hedge-school in a field close to the present school and arrived a year too late to meet an old woman who had sat at the feet of the hedge-schoolmaster. But I was compensated by having seen even this much in Carleton's Tyrone.

And in this district you can still hear vivid stories of the Great Hunger. One day in the parish of Termonamongin a farmer pointed across the glen to a grey church tower halfway up the other side. 'That's Old Magherakeel Protestant Church,' he said 'and there's a story about that churchyard that runs down to the river. In the days of the Famine they carried corpses to that churchyard from as far away as Donegal. They had to carry their dead across the River Derg at the ford—there was no bridge then—and ye can see the burying-place is on a brave steep hill. Well, when they got to below it, the bearers were so exhausted with the long journey they could go no further, and as many as eight corpses were lying at the bottom of the hill and the bearers not able to carry them up. My grandparents and the neighbours that was about here would come out and give them milk and oatcake, and when they had ate that, they were able to carry their dead up and bury them.'

Ballads are bred from memories such as this. In the next townland of Croighdenis I met John O'Donnell, whose childhood had been spent in a home that survived the Famine. And John, now well over ninety years of age, had a long rambling ballad about a wonderful potato, the *Ameriky White*, that was blight-proof, and so helped a remnant of the people of this valley to live through the catastrophe:

In the year '47, I'll tell yez of that,
There were bloodsuckin' merchants stored up their male,
They wouldn't sell any, their price was so canny,
They bared up their teeth like a dog goin' to bite.
Let them be aisy, I hope they'll run crazy,
Since we got the tattie, Ameriky White.

It was from John O'Donnell that I also heard *Barney McCann*, the story of how a racking landlord was frightened out of his wits:

There was a landlord of late,
He was wealthy and great,
And many an acre had he.
He caused his tenants to weep
For their cattle and sheep,
They were unhappy as creatures could be.
It was only a step to the poorhouse or grave
Once he gave them notice to quit.

The ballad relates how one tenant-at-will, Barney McCann, was given notice to quit because 'he had some good upland hay on the hill' that the landlord coveted for his bullocks:

> *Poor Barney was sad*
> *For he thought it too bad,*
> *After all his industry and care,*
> *To be robbed of his right*
> *In the open daylight,*
> *But the landlord was deaf to his prayer.*

The same doleful preamble could be heard in fifty other districts but the maker of this ballad gave it a twist that assured *Barney McCann* a long life at generations of hearthsides. For Barney beats the landlord and keeps his upland hay. He dresses up as Beelzebub and lies in waiting:

> *His owner so fair he was taking the air,*
>   *And the monster he chanced for to see;*
> *He ran while he could, but the divil pursued,*
>   *He stumbled, he fainted, he fell.*
>
> *When he came to, he says 'What are you?'*
>   *(For the man was half-dead in a fit)*
> *'I'm the Divil' says Barney 'And I've come*
>   *To give you notice to quit!'*
>
> *'Oh, what can I do for your Honour, for you?'*
>   *(For the man was half-dead with the fear)*
> *'Give Barney McCann a free lease of his land for 999 year!*
> *Come sign up the deed with all possible speed,*
>   *Or quickly prepare for to flit!'*
>
> *With a trembling hand he fulfilled the demand,*
>   *For there was no time to delay;*
> *The monster in black took it up in a crack*
>   *And these words unto him he did say:*

'If you ever again cause your tenants such pain,
  I'll leave you as dead as a nut,
For with me you will go to the region below,
  Where you'll never get notice to quit!'

I discovered, some time afterwards, that these lively
lines had been written by James O'Kane, the Bard of
Carntogher. In its journey of forty-odd miles from Co.
Derry to the Valley of the Derg the ballad had lost all
traces of its authorship. That, I believe, would have pleased
the Bard of Carntogher. Like William Allingham he heard
his own ballads sung through the twilight, and the singers
were unaware of the author.

'I never knowed anybody McCann around these parts,'
ventured an old man sententiously when John O'Donnell
had finished singing. 'And would it matter a damn if ye
did?' snorted another. Of course the second ancient was
right. It's a foolish man who goes looking for historical
accuracy in ballads. I found out, some time later, that the
Ameriky White potato was introduced to Ireland not in
1847 as the ballad says, but in the 1880s.

Who won the Great Battle of Magherafelt that incon-
venienced the citizens of that town between six and six-
twenty o'clock on the seventeenth of March, eighteen
hundred and seventy-three? There were, in fact, two
memorable victories, the Orange and the Green. The
Orange version relates how the Brethren:

. . . routed and utterly beat down
The Ribbonmen of Ardtrea, Bellaghy and Rocktown. . . .

We care not how these rebels roar or how their welkins ring
For the praises of our Orange Sons for evermore we'll sing.

The Green version is equally reliable:

Come all ye true bred Irishmen wherever that ye be,
I hope you'll pay attention and listen unto me,
Concerning a great victory gained with honour and renown;
Gained by the bold Bellaghy men and the heroes of Rocktown.

You pay your money, and if you're a wise man, you take the singer's choice.

Personally I'm all in favour of Party ballads. They've given us some of the raciest and most rousing of our Ulster songs. The Orange songs have about them a jauntiness that is almost entirely absent from the Green ballads. They also contain expressions of fraternal affection among the Orangemen which are very far from being as sentimental as they might appear. For The Orange Order, as a cohesive force, is of much greater significance to the Protestants, divided as they are into various denominations, than the Ancient Order of Hibernians is to the Roman Catholic laity. A part of this jauntiness (but not all of it) is due to the fact that the Orange ballad-makers stuck their words to melodies common in the Irish countryside.

The Protestant Drum goes to the tune of 'O'Rourke's Noble Feast'; the air of the *Boyne Water* is named, fittingly enough, 'Marcaidheacht na Boinne' (Cavalcade of the Boyne). One verse of the *Boyne Water* mentions a tune that every Ulsterman, whatever his favour, immediately associates with the Twelfth of July Walk:

He wheeled his horse—the hautboys played,
  Drums they did beat and rattle,
And Lilli-bur-lero was the tune
  We played going down to battle.

I'm not suggesting that 'Lillibulero' is an Irish air (some say that it was composed by Purcell), but its strange title is, proverbially, a parody of an Irish phrase. What that phrase was, like the origin of the melody, is still unsolved.

The *Boyne Water* has a musical affinity with the *Munster War Song*, a Nationalist ballad with an effective opening verse:

Can the depths of the ocean afford you not graves,
That you come thus to perish afar o'er the waves;
To redden and swell the wild torrents that flow
Thro' the Valley of Vengeance, the dark Aherlow?

But the turning of the phrase is self-conscious; the minor poet is at work here not the maker of ballads. The opening of the *Boyne Water* goes slap into battle:

July the first in Old-bridge town
  There was a grievous battle,
Where many a man lay on the ground
  By the cannons that did rattle.
King James he pitched his tents between
  The lines for to retire
But King William threw his bomb-balls in
  And set them all on fire.

The Nationalist ballads differ considerably in style not only from the Orange ballads but among themselves. The best of them are in the real story-telling tradition like

The Suit of Green or *The Patriot Maid* or the 1798 ballad
The Blarismoor Tragedy which:

> *Belfast may well remember*
> *When tyrants in their splendour,*
> *In all their pomp and grandeur*
> *Ride out to take the air.*

It is the story of four young militia men who are suspected
of conspiracy with the United Irishmen and are summarily
condemned and executed by 'wicked Colonel Barber':

> *The guns were then presented*
> *The balls their bosoms entered,*
> *While multitudes lamented*
> *The shocking sight to see.*

But a great number of Nationalist songs, particularly
those written in the nineteenth century, suffer from being
the produce of strenuous literary activity by political
movements like Young Ireland and Sinn Fein. From the
'literary' point of view they are better written and have
more feeling than the Orange songs, but the Orange ballad-
maker has more concern for his story and his characters.
When he has something to say he says it to the point, as in
the *Murder of McBriars*:

The whiskey it was in his head, no harm was in his mind,
He happened for to tell too loud the way his heart inclined.

(I could name one or two fat and portentous volumes
'analysing the Irish psyche' that say almost as much as that.)

It is a fair generalisation, I think, to say that the Orange
bards were concerned with their story and rather unhappy
when it came to evoking emotion in their characters,
whereas the Green ballad-writers when they sought to

tell a story were apt to wander off it and describe some
emotion which it aroused in themselves. Fortunately for
Ulster folk-song, these two characteristics are comple-
mentary. Between them they have produced balladry at
once virile and lyrical, spiritual and down to earth, and they
have wedded their words, almost exclusively, to airs in the
Gaelic mode.

★

Ever since the time of Edward Bunting (1773-1843)
nearly every collector of Irish music has prefaced his
published work with a doleful prophecy of the death of
folk-singing. But as they 'lowered down each coffined
song into its grave of cold print' they never seemed to have
recollected that some young fellow in an Antrim glen
or round by the lakes of Fermanagh was, at that very
moment, humming the tune as he had heard it from his
mother's lips. Tradition leaps the years, and a century of
folk-song becomes a mere span of two or three lifetimes.

That is why you can hear *The Plains of Waterloo* sung
with all the fervour of personal experience by old men whose
grandfathers fought against Bonaparte, and hear the lamen-
tations of a stricken people in the voice of men and women
whose parents hungered in 1847. Down in South Armagh
just recently I listened to a man singing *Shule Agra*—the
lamentation of a young girl whose lover had followed James
II into exile:

> *I would I were on yonder hill*
> *'Tis there I'd sit and cry my fill*
> *Till every tear would turn a mill*
> *Go dtillidh tu mo mhuirnin slan.*

> *I'll sell my rock, I'll sell my reel*
> *And then I'll sell my spinning wheel*
> *For to buy my love a sword of steel*
> *Go dtillidh tu mo mhuirnin slan.*

When the singer had finished he broke out passionately: 'That's about the Battle of the Boyne, James ran away and the poor fellas could do nothing but follow him!' For a moment the poor fellas were neighbours of his own. His song to him was more than history—it was part of his racial consciousness, and the Julys and Decembers of almost three centuries had but nurtured it.

Some time ago I had occasion to comment on the effect of a changing agricultural economy on the traditions of the countryside. A friend of mine, a fine ballad-singer, drew my attention to the passage. 'I wouldn't worry too much about that,' he said, 'down our way they're making up ballads about the tractor and the excavator just as their fathers made songs about the power-loom and the railway engine. That's the only difference between the old songs and the new—a different piece of machinery. The themes remain what they always were—love and anger and poverty and riches and the eternal struggle of the human spirit.' When I wrote the thing, I had in mind the disappearance of fairylore and harvest customs, but I accepted the mild rebuke as salutary and instructive.

The main stream of our Ulster folk-songs has its source in the Gaelic Irish tradition, but it has been enriched and widened by two important tributaries, Scots and English. In every county you'll hear songs that have their origin across the water: *Barbara Allen, The Jolly Ploughboy, The*

Dark-eyed Gypsies, Died for Love, The Green Beds. They are not always sung to their original airs but to some local modification of them or to tunes completely Irish. For our country singers either take an imported air and impress their character so strongly on it as to give it a native flavour, or—and this has happened just as often—they fall in love with the narrative of the ballad, neglect its original air, and substitute a favourite tune of their own. The *Ballad of Lady Margaret* is sung in Ulster to the air of 'The Green Autumn Stubble' and *Willie Taylor* does a slow dance to the tune of 'Finnegan's Wake'.

It may be indeed that dance rhythms, jig, reel or hornpipe, are the most prolific source of Ulster folk-songs. I'll let a bard from Strangford Lough have the last word on that. 'I always make my poems,' says he, 'to the lie of some good tune.'

Chapter Nine

TO CRACK BY THE HEARTH

I HAD A RELATIVE ONCE who could charm away the
'rose' or erysipelas. I don't know how he discovered this
gift in himself, for although any number of people have
walked across fields with hazel rods in their hands and never
felt as much as a quirk, few people, I should think, have
ever put themselves in the invidious position of experi-
menting on a sick neighbour without at least being licensed
to do so. It might have been a hereditary gift, but I doubt it.
Anyway, I shall never know now, for the healer is dead.
But undoubtedly he had the 'touch', so much so that in

the latter years of his life he had to feign sickness or weariness, or pressing work, to save himself long journeys over the midnight countryside.

He was also versed in what he called *legerdemain*, meaning by that stories and manifestations of the occult. I heard many such stories at his hearth, but the story I remember best, for he never tired of telling it, was about Toby Hunter and the cats.

'Many years ago (he said) when my father was a young fellow he was out one Hallowe'en night roaming the countryside for sport—and a very rough class of sport it was in those days, like blocking a man's chimney with sods and half suffocating the family or moving a stack from his haggard and rebuilding it in a haggard half a mile away. Anyway, the boys for devilment decided to visit the farm of Toby Hunter, a Roman Catholic neighbour. Toby got on very well with his neighbours, and if there had been any older men with these young fellows this story would never have needed the telling. Howanever, the boys were made welcome and invited in to join the family in the big kitchen.

'The night being what it was there was a certain amount of joking and mild horseplay around the fire, and young Mattie Hunter, the daughter of the house, soon became the centre of the fun. But when the horseplay became a bit too vigorous for Toby's liking he remonstrated lightly with the young fellows. He might as well have thrown his words up the chimney and in no time Mattie was squealing in real earnest. This time Toby had a sharp word to say and the answer was as sharp. Says Toby, "If ye don't quit tormenting the girl I'll gie ye a scare that ye won't forget in a while." Well, the odds of eight strapping young galoots to an old fellow don't encourage prudence and Toby was urged to go to the Warm Place. And then,' continued the story-teller, 'my father saw Toby Hunter thrust the tongs into the fire. They thought he was going to attack them and dispositioned themselves accordingly, for the truth was they had a drop of liquor taken. But what happened was worse and more than worse than what they had expected. Toby Hunter drew out the tongs right enough, but he never made to strike at anybody. He just spat on the hot metal and from wall to wall the kitchen filled with cats; big cats and wee cats, black cats and grey cats, brindled cats and ginger cats, all classes, makes, shapes and colours of cats. My father never drew breath nor let the heel of his boot touch the ground till he was in his own close a mile and a half away.'

'But surely,' said I, 'that sort of story was bound to gather round a man like Hunter—the only Catholic in the district?'

My relative bridled, 'Not at all,' he said sharply, 'Toby Hunter was only a very small wizard as wizards go. There were some first-class ones among the old Presbyterians in this very townland you're in now!'

He had missed the point of my query, but as we sat there rapt in mutual sectarian pride my curiosity was dissipated.

★

There is a belief, almost an article of faith, among Tin Pan Alley composers and others that the traditions of 'Old Ireland' are to be found only among citizens whose names are prefixed with 'O' and to a lesser extent 'Mac'; that is to say, the Roman Catholic population. As O'Flanagan, O'Hanagan and O'Lanigan are always good for a rhyme compared, say, to Craig, Poots or Mahaffy, this is very convenient for the song-writers. But in Ulster a man's surname is not a very reliable guide in deducing his religious persuasion; indeed it may be a very foolhardy one. An acquaintance of mine, Master of an Orange Lodge, bears a Milesian name to be found in the *dramatis personæ* of the Annals of the Four Masters. For all that he holds to the opinion, or rather the pugnacious certitude, that his name is a Dutch name inherited from a Dutch soldier who served in the armies of King William III. No one has thought it worth while to suggest to him that he might be under a misapprehension.

Nevertheless, it has been concluded by dance-band lyricists, hydroponic poets and writers of travel books (particularly writers of travel books who live in Dublin) that the traditions of Ulster can be found only in Catholic homes, because Catholics are more 'poetic', less 'materialistic'. I don't think this is so, indeed I consider it decidedly unfair to some very solid company directors I know, decent fellows all.

Nowadays the folklorist in search of material is more likely to find it in the mountainous regions than in the plains and valleys. In Ulster, for reasons which you will find in history, the mountainsides are inhabited by Catholics and the valleys by Protestants. Understandably, the old beliefs live longer among the scattered cottages in the hills than in the plump lowland acres tilled to the hedges

where the fairy thorns have been torn out and the souter-
rains filled in for the sake of a few extra bushels of grain.

In Ulster the pattern of custom and beliefs, the usage of
words and weapons, idiom and tools, suggest even to the
casual observer the contributions of different peoples and
traditions: Irish, Scots, English, Huguenot. Students have
told us much about the tools and utensils used by our
forefathers. Philologists have listed the words and idiom
borrowed and inherited, the lallans of Antrim and Down,
the speech of South Armagh and the Sperrins poured into an
ancient idiom, the Tudor phrase that glints in the bargaining
of the Tyrone farmer as sudden and delightful as a silver
coin in a handful of coppers. But no one, as yet, has unra-
velled all the threads of custom and superstition and traced
them back to the tongues and places of their origin. It is a
task of parfilage beyond the knowledge and ability of the
enthusiastic amateur. It demands the trained folklorist, or
better still, a body of them, a Folklore Commission set up
in the Province. And very soon he or they will be too late.

In an Ulster farm kitchen the family life radiated round the
fire rather than the table. The hearths were built for swinging
big feeding pots off the crane so there was ample space
around them for leg-room and conversation. The table was
usually thrust under the window or against the back wall.
Where the guest sat at table was not a matter of any great
significance but he was offered the place of honour at the
fireside, even the chair belonging to the head of the house,
which he just as politely refused.

Many country folk of a bygone generation never ate their
meals at the table but before the fire. There is the story of

an old woman of the Magherafelt district who used to seat
herself on the warm potato pot to eat her dinner of potatoes
and salt from the 'teemer' or wicker-strainer which lay
before her on the hearth. One day, when she mentioned
that she was failing in health, a friend demurred. 'Oh, but
I am,' declared the old lady. 'At one time the pratie-pot
was a perfect fit for me, but only yesterday I fell into it when
I was at my dinner!'

It would be a mistake to infer from this that the table was
of little importance in the Ulster farm kitchen. It was the
private and intimate place for family meals, and its deal
leaf scrubbed snow white was rarely if ever marked by the
cups and glasses of neighbours who had dropped in for a
'crack' or a *ceili*. There are many reasons why the hearth
predominated over the table as the centre of hospitality.
In a country with a damp climate it is much more pleasant
to sit at the fire than in the back end of a draughty kitchen.
Apart altogether from the question of abstinence there
was little or no beer drunk in the countryside, for beer,
cheese and yeast go together, and the open fire of the Ulster
farmhouse was unsuitable for baking yeast bread. The
Irishman ate little cheese (although two wars have made a
difference) and if he had a passing desire for the flavour he
could satisfy it with a taste of 'cheesy' butter, and was always
rather perplexed when the visitor found it distasteful.

When a bulky drink, other than tea, was required at the
meal table, buttermilk was served, and while no one enjoys
a glass of the stuff more than I do, I realise that there are
limits to the conviviality that may be engendered by a jug
of it. For generations the Irish have been copious tea

drinkers, and the query 'you'll take a cup of tea in your hand?' is as much a reminder of the seat at the hearth as it is a gesture of hospitality.

In my childhood I was fortunate enough to live for several years in the household of a small farmer, Alexander Gaw. Alexander was about seventy at the time, heavily bearded and his shoulders bowed by hard work. He divided his time between his five acres of land (or four, really, for one of his fields was marred by a whin knowe), and his harness-making business which he carried on in a lean-to at the gable of the house. His daughter 'took in flowering', that is to say, she acted as an agent for several of the linen firms in the city of Belfast, and distributed embroidery work to the needle-women of the district. These activities of the Gaws made their hearth a meeting place for their neighbours. In the evenings, when their day's work was done, the young men came with broken harness and wrenched buckles for Alexander's attention. The farm women, with their skirts kilted against the wet grass of the fields, would bring their finished embroidery. There was talk around the hearth of crops and markets, births and deaths, and if someone had brought a paper Alexander read it aloud, down to the (*Government Cheers*) and (*Opposition uproar*).

No one outstayed his welcome. When all the transactions had been settled the company rose to go. Several of the young men and women found that their homeward road lay over the same paths, and where they had arrived singly, or in twos, now a little cluster of lamps moved over the dark fields.

When the last neighbour had gone, supper was set on the table. Alexander usually had hot buttermilk, the rest of the family, tea. When the meal was finished Alexander took down the family Bible and read a few verses. It was now evident why the evening meal was delayed until the neighbours had gone. This hour was reserved for the dignity and privacy of the family. When the reading was finished the family knelt at their chairs and Alexander prayed. Experience had taught the younger members of the household to rise from their knees reluctantly, as it were, and to stifle any sigh of relief. Alexander could withdraw hand and eye from heavenly contemplation with devastating speed.

Apart from the Bible, which he read regularly but temperately, I can remember only three other books in which Alexander Gaw showed any interest. They were Emerson's Essays, *A Serious Call to a Devout and Holy Life* by William Law, and Robert Burns' Poems; and the only pages of the poet unthumbed was the glossary. He had a picture of the poet hanging on the wall beside the fireplace.

Alexander allowed himself few relaxations. But there was one event to which he looked forward with as much pleasure as the youngest member of his household, and that was the annual cockle-raking excursion. I can still recall the excitement as we hunted for the short-handled cockle-rakes among the couplings and rafters of the byres and sheds. Then when the rakes were found they had to be cleaned and the teeth of six-inch nails replaced where they were missing.

Usually four or five neighbouring families joined in the trip and shortly after breakfast, when the house had been redd up and the animals and fowl provendered for the day, all the family would pack into the trap and drive out to the main road where at each loanenhead we would be joined by our neighbours until a small cavalcade of traps would be moving along the winding road among the drumlins that led to Castle Espie on the shores of Strangford Lough.

Children are fickle labourers, as any parent knows who has tried to cajole a small son or daughter into helping him in the garden. We were no better; after a tentative scratching at the sands we gave up our cockle-rakes and ran off to the rocks to hunt for flounders or tear away pennants of leathery seaweed in search for dulce. But all over the flat dull sands our elders were stooped, with petticoats and trousers rolled to the knees, raking away and dropping the fat round shellfish into the potato bags they dragged behind them.

Then we were set to gathering twigs and driftwood for the fire that would boil the tea kettle, and as we all sat around on the sheep-cropped grass one of the women was sure to stroke her bare feet and sigh and thank God for an occasional paddle in salt water, and one of the men, brushing the crumbs from his moustache, was sure to say 'Aye, that's them washed for another year, Mrs McCoubrey!' and wink in such a way that we and Mrs McCoubrey and everybody else knew he was only joking, for such a joke, if mis-construed, might mean one trap load less at next year's excursion.

By the time the crockery was scoured with sand and

rinsed in a spring and the fire stamped out the lough was darkening, and the emerald glow fading from the Slave Rocks and The Island of Lost Sheep. A dripping sack of cockles was loaded on to the floor of each trap and in the rakers clambered, the women protesting, as usual, that their boots and stockings and skirts would be ruined on the cockle sacks.

When we got home we were sent across the fields to a neighbour's house with a calf's bucket of the shellfish. As everyone shared out there were cockles for supper in a dozen homes in the townland that evening. The big saucepan was put on the range or the pot hung on the crane and the cockles tipped in to stew in their own juice (some of the men would put two cockles hinge to hinge, unlock the shells and swallow the contents, but to boil the cockles first was the popular way to prepare them).

So far as our household was concerned the first sniff of brine had barely floated out of the pot when there would be a knock at the door and in would come the Man from the Lough and a crony (we children sitting patiently before our empty saucers and our buttered wheaten farl always hoped he wouldn't come *this* year, our elders knew better). The entrance and patter were always the same. He would take two steps into the kitchen, his eyes screwed up as though he were blinded by the light from the oil lamp, take a look at Alexander's Sunday collar, tie and gold watchchain, pause, take a step back and say 'Ach, I didn't know, Alec boy, have ye friends in?'

'Not at all,' Alexander would answer patiently, 'we're just back from Castle Espie. Come on in, the two of ye—'

'Ach now, Alec, we wouldn't like to do that! I was just out on my pad wi' James Orr here,' and he indicated a face glooming at us round the door like a harvest moon that had risen out of joint with the calendar.

'Well come in anyway, now that you're here and share a cockle.'

'W-e-e-l—' With murder in our eyes we watched him giving in with a good grace. 'Mebbe the wife was going to make an early night of it?' and he turned on her as false a smile as ever cracked a glutton's face. And Mrs Gaw, usually the most hospitable of women, would rattle the cockle pot angrily and cry, 'Will you come in for any sake and sit down! There's a draught blowing through that door would lift a bullock's feet off the floor.'

In they would come and sit down to rattling plates of cockles that by right of labour and inheritance were ours. And when they had finished and drawn their chairs up to the hearth we would fissle among their empty shells in the vain hope that one golden half moon had escaped engulfment under those ragged valances of moustaches.

Lying awake we listened to the bumbling drone of voices from the kitchen, the muted explosions of laughter, the chink of teacups. The talk would fall away into silence until someone would take up the story again, someone else would answer, and we would fall asleep to the antiphon of neighbours' voices round the hearth.

★

The Irish farmhouses, scattered over the countryside, seem as ancient as the hills and hollows on which they sit, but historians say that this pattern of isolated farms is comparatively modern and that many were hedged and fenced in the last century or so after the breaking up of the rundale system of farming and the dispersal of the barwins and clachans.

Four miles off the north-east coast of Antrim lies the island of Rathlin. Four miles, that is, as the sea-bird flies from Fair Head on the mainland to Rue Point on the island, but the small boat putting out from the port of Ballycastle has to sail in an arc of seven miles across the swift-running Rathlin Sound before it berths in Church Bay, at the principal landing-stage in the island. On Rathlin the visitor can still see the vestiges of the clachan community. If you pause on any high point of the road that wanders up the middle of the island you will see clusters of tumbled homesteads with their couplings bare to the sky. Most of these houses were deserted inside the last fifty years, for emigration has almost drained the island dry, at least, of its youth. The islandmen blame this on poor harbours both in the island and at Ballycastle, the mainland port. It is the old difficulty of communication; of travelling and returning, so important to an island community. When I was there, two years ago, a young farmer said 'why stay here labouring it out when the worst seven miles of salt water around the British Isles lie between my cattle and produce and the market square?' And another more bitterly: 'Even the women who are emigrating have to be hauled up by ropes at Ballycastle quay.' But they clung on here as long as they could, and when at last they were forced to leave, those who stayed on tore down the thatch from the empty houses to save the rates.

There are, of course, modern houses on the island. Good square houses with modern hearths and slated roofs and window-sashes; houses as neat and negative as any you'll find on the mainland. In an odd clachan an old house may still be occupied, so that in effect the Rathlin families live as isolated from each other as the farmers on the mainland. But as the mouldering clusters of walls crumble away under the winter gales they look as ancient as the seventh-century sweat house in the townland of Knockans. One young islander who had never known them occupied said to me: 'Ah, the old people lived close together in those days. 'Twas protection against the Danes and suchlike.' I discovered later that one of the clachans had been built and occupied by this lad's forefathers, but for three generations since the menfolk of his family had been emigrating and already the boy had difficulty in discerning the thread of continuity that bound him to this cluster of dwellings.

But one old man, Mr Mick Craig of Carravindoon, remembered when the earth floors of the ruins around his house were polished by the traffic of feet and the peep-o-day windows were glazed and fires of scraw turf and sea coal burned on the lichened hearthstones. I sat with him in his house and when we had finished our meal of fresh mackerel and barley bread we talked until the hour hand leaned forward on its face with sleep. He told me, among many other things, how the young men collected Hogmany Meal for the poor folk of the island.

'On New Year's Eve,' he said, 'all the young men of the

island would gather up, and they had horns, all they could get, and they blew through the horns together, and they had a bag with them, and they went right round from one house to another, you see, lifting meal for the poor of the island. They would go into a house and the people of the house threw a coal on the floor and in went the first young man with a sheepskin on his back, and another man behind him had a hold of the sheepskin and a stick in his hand to batter it with, and they marched in a circle round the coal and said this rhyme. . . .'

Mick still had the rhyme in the Scots Gaelic of the island, or at least most of it, and in English it runs something like this:

> Hogmanay, 'tis Hogmanay now,
> Here we come to sing our song now
> Here we come to dance again now,
> Here's the bag for the poor man's meal.
>
> Meal we look for in good measure,
> Fill the bag up at your leisure,
> What you give is still your treasure,
> God bless all whose home is here.
>
> God bless all whose home is here,
> And send you safe through all the year,
> Send you food and goods and gear
> And clothes to keep out wind and rain.
>
> May your friends be kind and true,
> May this coal burn each day new,
> Till again we visit you. . . .

'Then the man at the back of the sheepskin,' continued Mick, 'cut a bit off it and gave it to the people of the house as a receipt. And that bit of skin was put in the pot-crook at the hearth and kept there till the following New Year coming on—for to bring luck to the house. And when the people of the house had given the Hogmany Meal this was the wish that the young men left with them:

'That you may never die nor nobody kill you till the skin of a midge makes a nightshift for you. That you may never die in child-bed nor in any other bed; but in the open field where you'll have room to kick.'

In the small hours of the morning, when I had to leave Mick's hospitable hearth and return to my lodgings above Church Bay, he convoyed me down the loanen to where a ruin crouched among boretree and nettles. 'My grandfather helped to build that house,' he said, 'and before you go I'll tell you how it was built. There was a young fellow lived here in the townland of Carravindoon and he was going to get married and he had no house, nor habitation to take his wife till, and he asked all the young men of the lower end to the wedding, and they went to the wedding, and some took a spade with them and some took timber with them, and they started to build a house for him—and they built the house and they roofed it and put scraws on it and a grain of thatch, and that night they held the wedding in it and they were eating and drinking and dancing till the morning.'

As I left Mick and set off along the shore of Ushet Lough, the beam of the East Lighthouse brushed the hills, vanished, and left silence and darkness in the fields of Carravindoon. Many nights have passed since there was the light of hurricane lamps or laughter in these loanens; or a young man looking for house or habitation for his bride.

★

Several years ago I attended a country funeral. The July sun was as bold as brass that day and those who weren't relatives or near neighbours stood in the shadow of the rowans that fringed the close. At last the prayers in the house were finished and the coffin was carried out and set on the backs of two chairs to rest there until the first 'lift' to the hearse waiting up on the county road.

Four sons of the dead woman were to lift the coffin, and as they handed their hard hats to other mourners and bent to slide their shoulders under the coffin, a man beside me, a schoolmaster, whispered 'watch this', and as the coffin was lifted I saw an old man knock over one of the chairs with a dunch of his knee. It looked like clumsy old age. Then he pushed over the second chair.

'What's the idea in knocking the people's furniture about?'

'He's "trimmlin" the chairs; that's to say, he's making quite sure that the spirit of the departed hasn't gone to roost while the corpse is on its way to the churchyard.'

'Well, considering what we overheard through the parlour window either he or the clergyman has been misinformed.'

'I don't think the old man would see any contradiction there at all.'

'You mean he really doesn't believe in this "trimmlin" of his?'

'No, I wouldn't say that. I think it's just become a friendly superstitious gesture. Of course the young fellows laugh at him and I've no doubt he would say it's a lot of cod, too. But I've watched him at it, several times. Only it's made to look like an *accident* now, whereas in the old days the chairs were solemnly upended. . . .'

'How do you know that?'

'The old lady who's now in her coffin told me about it. She was a walking wonder for old stories and beliefs. This "chair-trimmlin" was a custom in her family, indeed among all the persuasion who attend the church we're going to this afternoon. I've never heard of it anywhere else, most certainly not in the parts I come from. But they had the "wake" there, with the wake-table, the drink, the baccy and the Lord-ha'-mercy pipes, and all the noise and ruction. I saw and heard it all when I was a kid. But around this locality nobody would ever dream of holding a wake for the dead.'

'I've never been to one. Were they as rowdy as people say?'

'Every bit.'

'Why?'

'It was the last wish of the departed—"a lively wake". And the relatives gathered to see that the wish was carried out even if it killed them—as it often did.'

'And how do you explain this townland custom of "trimmlin" the chairs?'

'I can't. I wouldn't even take my oath that it isn't known in other parts of the country. At one time it might have been a widely practised superstition that has disappeared except from corners like this. And remember, there are variants of it, like shrouding the mirror in a death-room. . . . Look, if you just stand aside here we'll join the end of the line. The vet. promised us two seats up to the church. . . .'

★

Looking back over this chapter, I see that some of the stories and customs I have mentioned are rather beyond the flicker of the fire. The explanation of this is not hard to come by, for the notes and notions that I intended grouping round the country hearth came forward dragging by the hand incidents that I had forgotten. Two other such recollections come to mind and I think this is as good a place as any to set them down.

The custom of cutting the last scythe-clasp of corn and plaiting it into a *cailleach* or *granny* or *churn* is still well known throughout Ireland. In Alexander Gaw's house this symbol of good luck was known as the *churn*. But once it had been carried home and hung between the shot horns on the varnished wall of the porch, and a high tea had been served to the reapers, the harvest festivities were finished so far as the farmhouse was concerned. But in Tyrone, in the district beyond Killeter, the rejoicing for a good harvest is a much more neighbourly affair. This is how a little girl described it to me:

'My Dad was in great good humour because he was first with his corn. He told mother we would have a spree. Mother and all of us got busy cleaning and redding-up.

The barn was swept of all cobwebs and made nice-looking. Hurricane lamps were hung from the roof and a platform made from bars and planks. This was all done by the neighbour lads. My mother and neighbour ladies were busy cooking in the house. Some were baking oven scones, corn cakes and oatcakes; others were roasting and boiling fowl; and others made jellies and nice things.

'As it was getting dark, the farmers with their wives, sons and daughters came along. Some were specially invited, and others came without an invitation, but all were made welcome. The pipers and the fiddlers out in the barn struck up a lively tune, and before five minutes, the barn floor was full. Some were dancing on the street, others in the kitchen. It was lucky the moon was rising, I heard my father say. As the dance went on, mother thought it would be better to get on with the supper, so Dad invited those nearest the house to come in first, and about two dozen were able to sit down at the tables in the room and the kitchen, until everybody got their fill.'

It was a man from the shores of Lough Neagh who told me about the custom of Baking the Frog Bread. The district in which he lives, Moyola, was at one time a centre of hand-loom weaving. But the introduction of the power-loom put an end to that. The small farmer-weaver had the choice of following the new factories into the towns or leaving the country altogether and emigrating, usually to America.

Irish tenors in crisp boiled shirts have succeeded in turning the Irish emigrant with his hanky bundle and his heartbreak into a sentimental whimsy. It is in the letters from the emigrants and in the half-forgotten ballads of the countryside that we hear the anger and anguish of parting from their native place and learn of the horrors of the emigrant vessels. The Frog Bread was baked and eaten as a protection against the diseases that killed so many wanderers:

'In the old days when times were bad,' said the story-teller, 'there was a great number of young boys and girls emigrated to America from this district of Moyola.

'Going to America in those days was looked upon as being the final parting, and the young emigrants spent their last fortnight visiting all their friends and relations in the district.

'Well, of course they wouldn't be allowed out of any house without a cup of tea and a bite to eat, and it was during these meals that they were given, unbeknownst to them, a piece of Frog Bread.

'This Frog Bread was a protection against all foreign diseases like cholera, yellow-fever or small-pox. I'll tell you how the Frog Bread was made. The woman of the house would catch a frog, open it and clean it just like a chicken. It was then roasted, indeed over-roasted, and ground into a fine powder. This powder was dredged into a handful of flour and baked into a farl of bread on the griddle. And then the young lad or lass would be given a piece of it to eat. The reason the frog was picked was because of its cleanliness, for it feeds and thrives on God's holy dew of the dawn.'

Perhaps the Harvest Spree and the custom of eating the Frog Bread have not moved so far away from the country fireside. There are impulses behind these customs difficult to discern, but even the most casual observer cannot help but note the hospitality, the generosity, the concern for a neighbour's well-being. And these pleasant attributes are still present in the farm-kitchen when Ulster country folk gather to crack by the hearth.

Summer Loanen

and other stories

by

SAM HANNA BELL

THE MOURNE PRESS

Newcastle, Co. Down

MCMXLIII

CONTENTS

SUMMER LOANEN

THE boy in the corduroy kneebreeches moved slowly down the sunny gnat-hung loanen, searching the sheughs for sourleek or wild strawberries. He turned each leaf carefully before he put it in his mouth, since the afternoon on Quinn's knowe when he had felt a little slippery body under his tongue.

The feathered quicken-grass and nodding goose-grass with its wheatlike head grew into the loanen, making shaded arbours between the ancient blackthorn roots. It was the vivid crimson jersey of the boy which caught the strawberry hunter's eye. He sat with his back to the ditch, cushioned on the lush grass, and he juggled three white stones, letting them run through his fingers and fall on the ground between the crook of his chubby knees.

Although he could not have failed to hear the approach of the other, the boy on the bank did not raise his head. He seemed engrossed in lifting and tossing his polished pebbles, and all that the newcomer could see of his features were a tangled sphere of light sunbleached hair, the perspective of round ruddy cheeks, a snub nose appearing and disappearing behind his forehead fringe as he raised and lowered his head with the juggling stones, and a glimpse of a sturdy sun-reddened neck.

Around the ankle of the boy in the red jersey was fastened a goat-collar and from it ran a long tether into the heart of a boretree bush. The boy approached the seated figure, and squatting down, cried in a friendly but excited voice, ' Hi, wee lad, ye're tethered tae the dyke ! ' The long grass stirred a little distance away and a little girl stumbled out of the hedge backwards, her soiled chubby hands full of the stemless heads of daisies, wild violets and lady-fingers.   She approached the two boys, and after staring fiercely at the intruder, she turned to the seated boy. ' Spit on him, Jimmie,' she said.

The boy in the corduroy breeches stepped back, intimidated by this reception. " What wud he want tae spit on me fur," he protested, " sure I never did ye ony harm ? "   Then with an ingratiating smile he continued, " What are ye tied like that fur, wee lad ? "

The boy still remained with his eyes on the ground, his cheeks perhaps a shade darker, the white stones motionless on the grass.   The little girl put her foot with its square-toed boot in the crotch of a bush and swung her knee.   " It's because he wet the bed ! " she said.

The boy in the corduroy breeches gave an incredulous " heh ! "   " Jimmie," the girl appealed, " didn't Gramma tether ye fur wettin' the bed ? "

" Ye think ye're quare an' funny, wee girl," said the boy in the corduroy breeches. For answer the girl threw back her head, pursed her lips, and spat violently in the direction of the sceptic. Her expectoration was more violent than scientific, for all that appeared was a fine spray which fell through the warm air on the bended head of her brother.

For the first time the boy on the ground spoke. " Girls are no good of spitters," he said, wiping his cheek. At this treachery his sister gave an indignant cry, and raising her foot delivered him a solid kick on the

haunch, then turned and fled down the loanen, her short
serge skirt tearing at the seeding grass.

The boy on the ground nursed his leg, gazing after the
fleeing figure of his sister. " Wull ye help me tae catch
her ? " he asked the other. " I wull that," answered
the boy in the corduroy breeches. " We'll throw her in
the linthole," said the boy on the ground. " Ach, no,"
said the other, " sure we micht drown her."

Jimmie got up, removed the collar from his ankle,
pulled up his stockings and nodding to the boy in the
breeches, set off after his sister. He moved with a roll,
slow but strong, his heavy bottom jutting as he ran.
The other boy was lighter and swifter, accelerating
where the grass was thin, running close on the other's
heels.

At a gap in the hedge Jimmie stopped. " There she
is," he said, " crossin' owr the bog meadow. Go you
roun' by the tap an' kep her till I catch her." The
other boy nodded and jumped over into the field. He
had run a few paces when Jimmie called him back. " Hi,
boy, what dae they call ye ? "

" Francie McCoy."

" I'm Jimmie Orr an' her name's Nannie Orr. She's
my sister. Now you kep her in frae the tap."

In a few minutes they had so overhauled and surrounded the little girl that she retreated to the top of a
fallen yellowed hayrick where she stood swaying pre-
cariously, a sod in each hand, shouting defiance. With
a wild whuroo her brother rushed the stronghold,
catching an ill-aimed missile as he ran, and gaining the
top flung himself down at her feet with a laugh, rolling
over on his back with his face to the sun. Francie

dropped his outstretched arms, greatly relieved that he had not actually to grapple with the defiant young termagant. He approached the rick as Jimmie invitingly patted the warm straw. " Wur ye in earnest aboot throwin' her in the linthole ? " he asked.

Jimmie threw back his head and laughed. " Ach, I wus only jokin'!" He stretched up to stroke his sister's tumbled fair hair as she knelt between the boys. " Sure I wudn't throw Nannie in the hole fur ony money." Nannie's head bent to her brother's caressing, then straightening up she said to Francie with pointed emphasis, " We cud throw you in the hole."

Suddenly Jimmie slipped down to the sharp elastic stubble. " Come on, we'll mak bows an' arris an' hunt ! " Although Francie and the sister were but a few feet away, he bellowed his words, a crimson figure against the ashy stubble, waving his arm imperiously like a commander rallying a cavalry charge.

The golden wands swayed and fell as a muddy heel or strong fingers tore at them close to the water's surface. Jimmie snapped the frond heads and tossed them to Nannie. Francie and he notched the ends and strung them, then with blackhead reeds as arrows they went hunting.

But the osiers were young and green and full of sap, and after a pull or two they straightened slowly like a tired goat's leg and the reed slithered harmlessly over the grass. " D'ye know what my Grandpa says ?" said Jimmie, throwing his bow on the ground, " he says if you tuk a good ashplant there, an' put it in the chimley tae dry, and then strung it wi' a thong, ye cud drive a sally rod through a byre dure wi' it."

" Aye, an' maybe kill a baste," said Francie laughing.

A look of exasperation came on Jimmie's face. Ye're a quare silly wee fella, Francis. Sure ye'd tak the bastes out before ye'd dae ony firin'."

" D'ye go tae ony school, Francie McCoy ?" asked Nannie.

" Nane ava, but I'm goin' after the harvest."

" D'ye think ye'll be goin' tae Ballyilveen School where ould Master Rankin is ?"

" Ma father wants me tae go tae a town school."

The Orrs lay back on their elbows and looked at him. Idly Francie picked up one of the discarded bows, unstrung it and cast it along the grass. Immediately Jimmie was on his feet. " Spears is just as good as arris. We'll go huntin' wi' spears." " We'll go," said Nannie in a thrilled whisper, " tae Master Rankin's diamon' and hunt his goat."

Admiration, affection and excitement passed over Jimmie's face as he gazed at his sister. " Nannie," he said, " ye're a quare wee girl." Then he set off across the field, thrashing his thigh with an osier, in search of Master Rankin's goat.

They came on the goat cropping quietly under the lea of the hedge which ran around the little diamond-shaped field. Every few seconds she would shake her bearded head free from the clegs and flies which sipped at the rims of her old eyes. " Watch !" breathed Jimmie. His wand sped through the hedge, bounced on the razor-like spine of the goat and ricocheted into the field. The goat jumped with a clatter of its tethering-chain, her head lowered to the hedge. At the same time a man

in soiled riding breeches and unbuttoned waistcoat
sprang on top of the dyke, clutching the bushes with one
hand to steady himself and brandishing a billhook in the
other. " G'wan, ye wee whelps ye !" he shouted.
" Ah, it's you, Jimmie Orr, I'll teach you to maltreat a
poor beast of a goat ." He sprang over the hedge and
stooping down picked up a stone and flung it after the
fleeing children. He hitched, as a countryman does,
from the waist, and the missile hummed over Francie's
head like an angry bee.

" It was oul' Rankin brerdin' his hedge," gasped
Jimmie as they breasted the steep slope of the grazing
field. The man continued to shout threats after them,
his last shot reaching their ears as they disappeared over
the slope, " I'll tell your Grandma you're skiltin' the
fields with a papish, my bold Jimmie Orr !"

They reached the little loanen, shadows gathered in
the nooks of its old gnarled hedges, the insect sounds
dissolved and gone in the cool evening air. Jimmie
squatted down and reached in the grass for his white
stones. Nannie shivered, and said she was going to
bring in the ducks. " Can I come too ?" asked Francie.
She looked at him coldly and passed by without reply.
Francie hung around watching Jimmie as he scrubbed a
blood-spangled knee with spittle and a docken leaf.
At last he ostentatiously buttoned his jacket," So long,
Jimmie," he said. " So long, wee fella," answered
Jimmie, without raising his head.

A shrill cry halted Francie in his path. Nannie had
climbed on the farm-close gate, a finger pointed at the
distant Francie. She lowered her voice when she saw

her brother's head bobbing up the loanen hedge. " Tell that wee fella to come over an' play the morra," she said. Francie heard and waved his hand in reply. " I wull, Nannie, I wull !" he shouted. Then he turned and rushed down the dusky loanen, kicking madly at the dew-heavy grass in his delight.

BOUND LIMP CLOTH

THERE's a trick to spinning off a frocklength of georgette or marocain at one turn of the wrists. Most good drapers' assistants like Eugene can judge it pretty accurately. After all, he had been at it, if you include his apprenticeship, for about ten years.

During that time he had risen by the normal geologic process from apprentice to second assistant in the Dress Department of Messrs. Hamilton's. In his apprentice days he had been sent out to wholesale houses for cards of button-holes, and in later years he had squabbled with the buyer as to who should brush the Department floor. In short, " he was experienced in handling all classes of materials, and had a good grasp of the trade."

One of Eugene's special duties was to replenish the stock from the upstairs stockroom. It was during one of these visits that he came across the Little Library of the World's Greatest Books ; it sat, complete in twelve volumes, in a dusty corner of the room. The Library had been purchased, in all innocence, by Miss Boomer, the buyer of the Book Department. She had been in the Corsets and Girdles until the incongruity of her figure had compelled Mr. Hamilton, a gentleman of business acumen and delicacy, to have her moved into the Books.

Eugene blew the dust off the first volume, and opening it, stumbled with Jean Valjean through the catacombs of Paris. Half an hour later, he heard Bobby the apprentice, shout his name. Dreamily, Eugene put the book back into the fixture, and lifting the web of voile, returned to his department. But he was back again in the afternoon, and soon the stockroom, to which he had always mounted in a spirit of weariness, became his haunt.

Literary study during business hours is generally not encouraged by large drapery firms. When Mr. Magroarty, Eugene's boss, who was under the impression that Eugene spent his time cuddling an assistant from the Fancies in the stockroom, heard that he was wasting his time reading, his indignation and disgust knew no bounds. A request, an ultimatum, that he should make up his mind whether he was an assistant in the Dresses or a ruddy professor, decided Eugene. He started to take the books home, one by one, and place them on his bookshelf. He told no one of this, not even his girl-friend, Miss Turley, Mr. Hamilton's typist. If he thought of it all, he felt that he was taking home Mr. Pickwick, Corporal Trim and Becky Sharp from the dust of the stockroom into the brightness of his kitchen. The theft, if theft it was, was as amoral as a goat eating a rose.

Doubtless the Little Library might have sat in the stockroom until it disintegrated in dust, but when the last volume had disappeared a hue and cry was sounded through Messrs. Hamilton's. It was Bobby the apprentice, who split on Eugene. Mr. Hamilton, wise in the ways of pilfering employees, gave Mr. Magee, assistant cashier, the day off to investigate in the book-stalls of Smithfield Market. Mr. Magee, knowing Eugene better than did Mr. Hamilton, went to the

young man and questioned him on the missing volumes.
" Of course," replied Eugene, " I have them at home.
I'll bring them back when I've finished *The Fortunes of
Nigel.*" " Don't throw it around you," said Mr.
Magee, with mordant wit, " for you've got yourself into
a helluva jam." Then he went out and had his lunch
at the firm's expense, attended the afternoon matinee at
the Hippodrome, and returning at five o'clock, told Mr.
Hamilton that he had located the books in Eugene's
house.

" Send the young man in to me," said Mr. Hamilton.
As he awaited Eugene, he consulted the Black Record
in which all the misdemeanours of every soul in
Hamilton's were recorded. Against Eugene's name it
was written down that he had broken a yardstick in the
third year of his apprenticeship, but he had not, so far
as Mr. Hamilton could see, been implicated in any theft,
arson or Trade Union activity.

" But I wasn't going to sell them, sir ! " declared
Eugene, when Mr. Hamilton taxed him with the theft.
" It was the people I took for awhile." He took a
steadying breath. " They were books, I suppose, but
it was the people—Mr. Pickwick, you know, and
Quesauomda, and—and then I was going to bring them
back " he finished lamely.

" I see " said Mr. Hamilton, coldly.

" I'm afraid that sounds mad, but I saw them as
people . . ."

" My dear young man, you don't seem to see this—
this lapse of yours, I suppose we must call it, in its
proper light," exclaimed Mr. Hamilton angrily. " No
one is interested in the contents of the books here, what

we are trying to get at, is that you took articles from this firm which were for sale. For a man of your age, you seem to have a very elementary idea of property. Property " said Mr. Hamilton " is sacred. Not sacred in the wishy-washy sentimental way that some good people talk about certain things, but really sacred. Oh, I keep abreast of the times," said Mr. Hamilton, with raised forefinger, " I know the trend of modern thought. But there's one thing that you fellows seem to forget. If people like me didn't put our money and our energy into building up businesses, how would people like you get jobs ? Eh, Mr. Melady ? "

" And if people like me didn't work in your shops, sir, how would people like you have money ? " asked Eugene.

Mr. Hamilton turned a dull red. " Come, come, young man, enough of this. I have wasted some time explaining the Sacred Rights of Property to you. Your parents or your clergyman should have done so, they're expected to do so."

" It was foolish of me to take the books sir," said Eugene humbly.

" It was " agreed Mr. Hamilton, " very foolish indeed. " I may say," he continued, tapping the Black Record, " that your record here has hitherto been satisfactory. You are obviously a young man of parts, not perhaps gifted with those talents best suited to the drapery trade, but still a young man of intelligence. Have you ever thought of any other vocation, the ministry for example ? "

" No, sir," replied Eugene.

Mr. Hamilton gazed at him for a second. " Very

well, wait outside, Mr. Melady, and send in Mr. Magee."
When Mr. Magee arrived Mr. Hamilton asked him how
much Eugene was paid. " Thirty-five shillings a week,
and ten shillings average weekly commission " answered
Mr. Magee promptly.

" And the cost of the books were one and sixpence
each," continued Mr. Hamilton, figuring on his blotter.
" That is for the twelve volumes, eighteen shillings, a
little soiled, I believe, say fifteen shillings." Mr.
Hamilton laid down his pencil. " Give Mr. Melady a
note to the cash office for one pound ten shillings, and a
receipt for fifteen shillings. Doubtless he will find some
post with greater scope for his studies than Hamilton's."

" Yes, sir," answered Mr. Magee, laughing heartily.

Who can describe the emotion which filled the bosom
of Miss Turley, on hearing these words ? Throwing
down her rubber, she hastened across the office to Mr.
Hamilton's desk. " Sir," she said, " I feel that this is
an intrusion, but I would ask you to reconsider the
decision advised in yours of the last. Mr. Melady, I
know, is keenly interested in books. May I suggest that
you consider him for the buyership of the Book Department, because Miss Boomer, as you know, sir, is retiring
shortly to a job in her sister's post office." She stood
before Mr. Hamilton, supplicating yet proud. What
will a woman not dare for the man she loves ?

" You are in love with this young man ? " asked Mr.
Hamilton with a kindly twinkle.

" Yes, Mr. Hamilton," breathed Miss Turley,
blushing.

" And do you think he would stop this reading nonsense if you were married ? "

" Yes, Mr. Hamilton," said Miss Turley, clearly.

" Very well. Tell Mr. Magee that the previous instructions are cancelled. Mr. Melady is to be entered in the wages book as the buyer of the Book Department. His salary is to be increased to two pounds five shillings per week, and of course, as with the other buyers, no commission."

" Oh, Mr. Hamilton, how can I thank you ! " cried Miss Turley. Tears sparkled in the happy girl's eyes.

Mr. Hamilton waved her away. " Nonsense, my dear," he said. If his staff was happy and contented, that was reward enough for Mr. Hamilton.

And now instead of drifting along, questioning, uneasy, independent, Eugene is a sensible married man, and grows daffodils and beans in a plot on the Lagan Embankment.

ALWAYS RAISE YOUR HAT TO A HEARSE

MANY elements lend to the beauty of mellow thatch. The birds ; the furtive gleam of lichen at the gables ; the swallow's dark cavern beneath the eaves ; the vagaries of weather ; rain subduing the oaten gloss ; smoke falling in patches of umber below the chimneys. The skilled craftsman who lays the straw and binds it against the winds with osier scobes provides the human element. In Gortmoyle that element went by the name of Banjo Reilly.

A fine craftsman, Banjo Reilly, a thinker, a man who had pondered deeply the age-old dilemma, whether a man should keep friends or keep money. To his own satisfaction Banjo had solved it, for he had many friends. He had a cottage, a bicycle with dropped handlebars, and a wife whose flowering on hoops was a miracle of embroidery.

But the good repute of Banjo was not bound by the townland of Gortmoyle. He was a crony in the lanes of Ardglass, a figure in the cathedral city of Downpatrick, a name in Belfast. There is little thatching now in Ardglass, and less in Downpatrick and Belfast, but porter, porter as Banjo once declared in McBurney's pub, in the course of an impassioned speech on Land Annuities, porter is universal.

It was Banjo's custom, it was a tradition in Gortmoyle, that when he had worked steadily for a month or more, he would disappear and not a hair of him be seen, till he stepped into his kitchen, maybe a week later, to kiss his wife, placid Teresa, and call for his supper. He would rise on a sunny morning, throw his leg over his bicycle, and ride away. He's away, Teresa would say, seeing through the little kitchen window that he had neither rope nor thatching-knife on his back. I'll clean out the parlour, or maybe, I'll whitewash the outhouse. The boyo's off again, the farmers would observe as he passed them on the market road, and they would call after him that their byre-roofs might need looking at on his return.

He had cycled away again, this June morning, Teresa had shouldered her solitary rounds, and Gortmoyle its immemorial dying and conceiving.

On the afternoon of the next day a lorry clanged out of a side street in Belfast, and for all the driver's frenzied skill, ran down and crushed a man riding a bicycle with dropped handlebars.

As the body was being lifted into the ambulance, a man leaned forward and gazed into the mutilated face. " B'gob, it's Banjo Reilly ! " he exclaimed. A shawly woman at his elbow called to the policeman, " Hi, here's a man knows the dead fella ! " The constable closed his notebook and pushed his way through the gaping crowd. " Are ye acquainted with the victim av the accident ? " he asked the man. " I shud be," the onlooker replied, " he's married on a sister av mine, an' lives at Gortmoyle, beyont Downpatrick." The shawly woman turned to the crowd, " God help the poor cratur, he was married on a sister av this man's, an' comes from beyont Downpatrick." " Ah, God help him," the crowd sighed in response.

" Will ye come down to the morgue and indentify

him officially ? " the constable asked the man. The man agreed and clambered into the cab of the ambulance beside the policeman and the driver. The brother-in-law's name was Malachy Toal. There is à Malachy Toal in every family ; a death, a foaling, a family feud, and he comes into his own. When he had identified the deceased, he caught the first bus to Gortmoyle, broke the news to his sister, called at the priest's house, arranged for the grave to be opened, and returned to Belfast with Teresa's signature on the burial insurance papers.

They gave Banjo a grand funeral. Walking behind him on his last journey were men from the butt of Louth, men from Tyrone, men from as far as Carnlough on the coast road. Thin-faced strangers in moleskins with ashplants in their hands would appear over the little white hills leading down to Gortmoyle, begging heaven to succour them in their grief when they were within earshot of Teresa's home. They poured into Gortmoyle all that day, and those who were late for the funeral lingered for the mourning.

The burial money was in the neighbourhood of sixty pounds, and Teresa spread it in lashings on the wake. For two days and two nights Gortmoyle mourned Banjo Reilly. There was weeping and dancing, courting and fighting. There was a great quantity of drink consumed. On the eve of the third day the mourners went down with the sun, over the little white roads from Gortmoyle.

On the evening of the fifth day after his interment, Banjo pushed open his door, skimmed his cap adroitly across the kitchen, and caught Teresa as she fainted into the hearth. " Woman dear," he cried, as she opened

her eyes, " what have ye been doin' atall ? " his eyes
taking in the brown bank of bottles in the corner. " Ah,
Micky, ye're dead, ye're dead ! " cried Teresa wildly,
" sure we've been buryin' ye an' wakin' ye fur two
nights now. It was wee Malachy Toal came down here
with a corpse claiming to be you, a fine body of a man
with the arr of a boil on its throat just my dear Micky,"
and Teresa laid her head on Banjo's shoulder and wept.

The hilarity of Banjo on hearing of his death and
burial, resounded through Gortmoyle and the kitchen
filled rapidly with neighbours reproaching themselves
good-naturedly on their little faith. " I tell ye what,
Banjo," cried big Hami Gaw, " b'God boy, ye're
immortal ! " He had voiced the opinion of the kitchen.

" An' were ye all at my funeral ? " cried Banjo,
shaking his head and choking with laughter. " Every
man av us, every man av us," answered one. " There
wus one that wusn't," said a little man from the shadow
of the dresser. " Shuey Ogle wusn't there." " Now
ye're right there, boy," conceded the first speaker. " He
telt me," continued the little man, " he wus takin' the
powny an' trap tae Crossgar tae bring back his son, fur
he said by the look av the scum that had gathered intae
Gortmoyle fur the funeral, he wud be needin' his help
in the bar."

Banjo was on his feet, his face livid with anger.
" Did he by God ! " he cried, and darting across the
room he seized his thatching-knife and rushed out of the
house. From down the street came the distant crash
of breaking glass, a woman's scream, and then the sound
of men's voices raised in anger.

Banjo was standing in the moonlit street, his arms

stretched out to a nightgowned figure in a broken window over the pub. " Come down ye slimy stoat till I put my hands on ye," he cried. " My money wus welcome when I wus livin', but when I wus dead ye hadn't the common grace to see me buried. Gimme back my thatchin'-knife, ye thievin' rascal ! "

" Ye bloody murderer, ye," cried the publican, " ye near cut the head aff my wife ! "

A wicked smile glowed on Banjo's face. " I'm what ye wudn't understand, Shuey Ogle. I'm a christian. I repay ye good fur evil." With a gesture of disdain he swung on his heel, and was received into the joyous bosoms of his friends.

TWO BLADES OF GRASS

" You'll have to show yourself " my wife said.
" Why ? " I asked. " I don't know them—and anyway,
look at the colour of my bowler, its bottle-green." Oh, it
looks all right," said my wife, " and, anyway they were
good to us that week-end at Bangor." " But that's
years ago, 1936 or something ! " " Well " said my wife
stubbornly, " the mother is a cousin of mine." " Now
that's something " I said, rather bitterly, " *that's* a very
good reason. Did you even know the girl ? " " I saw
her once, when she was a child," answered my wife.
" What age was she when she died ? " I asked. " About
nineteen, I think " my wife said. " You will go, wont
you ? " " Oh, I suppose so," I grumbled. " It means
taking an afternoon off from the office, remember."
" Well, just walk a little distance with them. I'm sure
that'll be all right."

" What's the father's name ? " I asked at lunch-time
the next day. " Bob " said my wife. " If I ask for
Bob, then ? " I said, reaching for my hat. " Yes. He's
bound to remember you. Here, let me brush you." I
had to run back to the house, after all. " What's the
number in Ankara Street ? " " Fifty-something, at the
Shankill Road end. But you'll see the carriages and
things outside the house."

As I walked round Ankara Street corner two elderly
men in bowler hats and black ties came out of a
tobacconist's shop. One of them had a twenty packet

of Gallagher's in his hand, and the other one, the shorter one in shapeless sewer-pipe trousers, was raising his hand expectantly towards the box. If they light up, I thought, the funeral must be further down the street. The man with the cigarettes put one in his mouth, and gave one to his companion.

Apart from godwillsits like starvation and war, I thought, its frightening to think that people can die at nineteen. When old people die we don't panic. It seems natural. If it was simply a matter of good taste, I thought, some of us might jump off a bridge at thirty. But not at nineteen, and not if its a woman. No woman is ugly both inside and outside at nineteen, and God knows we could do with all the beautiful insides we've got. That's what I was thinking as I followed the little man in the sewer-pipe trousers. Therefore it was safe to assume that this girl would have a boy. I felt sure I could spot him just by the look on his face. Suddenly I looked up, and there were the carriages.

The two men pushed their way through the crowd of urchins at the door, and I hurried forward and followed at their heels. A little boy detached himself from his friends, and I heard him mimicking me up the hall. When I turned, he screamed with laughter, and rushed out to his companions.

I walked into the little dark hot kitchen. The light was broken up by the heads and shoulders of people who were standing and people who were sitting along the walls. I found a place to stand at the scullery-door. A woman was leaning against the scullery sink, and another sat on the table opposite her, swinging her legs. The woman on the table, the younger one, was telling the woman against the sink about a party she had been to in this house. I turned and looked into the kitchen. Before me on a sofa sat a row of old women. In the corner, between the sofa and the range, sat an old man, his hands clasped on the head of a stick. He had an awed smile on his lips, like a country child, who, for the first time sees a great expanse of moving water. Close to the range, with a shawl over her head, sat an old woman. There was a hum of talk over everything.

As I stood leaning against the doorpost a woman gave me a cup of tea with a buttered abernethy biscuit in the saucer, to warm me. A man in the corner by the hall-door was protruding his stomach so that another man could examine the medal hanging from his watch-chain. " . . . . . bate Ballyclare Comrades in the final, two t'nil." He let his stomach sink with a proud sigh. The girl on the scullery table was still talking of the party. " . . . . . and Willie, the silly cratur, was that mad when he saw Florrie sittin' wi' the English soldier he wudn't come out av the scullery. Ye know the way he usta sing an' get on—but now the English fella was doin' all the singin' ! " One of the old women on the sofa was eating the biscuits from other people's saucers. She would snatch the biscuit, and push it, almost whole, into her mouth. When it seemed that her old cheeks would tear, the pressure of her gums would break it, and her face would collapse into a mumbling pouch. " . . . . . an' Willie, sittin' there like death warmed up. So I comes down an' I ses ' sure its no show without Punch, Willie, come on up an' give us a laugh.' ' All right, Maggie ' he ses, an' the silly fool jumps up an' lifts down that enema syringe an' puts the nozzle in his mouth, an' the bulb below

his arm, an' marches up into the kitchen lettin' on to be a
bagpiper. God, ye shud a heard that kitchen! An' ye
shud a seen Florrie! She rolls up against me with the
tears flyin' down her cheeks. ' Maggie ' she gasps,
' Maggie, fur God's sake stop him. I'm wettin' meself! '
Poor fella, he was killed in Scotland a coupla months later,
an' min' ye, Florrie Mahood felt it. . . . . ." The old
lady's eyes had drooped. She belched slightly and
patted the crumbs from her rusty bosom.

I went across and spoke to the man with the football
medal. " Is Bob about ? " I asked. " Ye'll get him
upstairs, more'n likely " he said. I thanked him and
mounted the stairs to the top landing where I paused
uncertainly. Through the open door of the front room
I saw the head of the coffin and a woman leaning over it.
I heard the low voices of others in the room. The
woman saw me, and came out with a sad smile. " Is
Bob here ? " I asked. She looked about vaguely " He's
not here," she said, " he must be downstairs, in the
parlour, maybe." As I turned to go, she caught my
sleeve. " Would you like to see her ? " she asked. I
didn't know what to do. I wanted to say that I would
rather remember her as I last saw her. The woman was
looking at me. I nodded. She led me into the room, and
the two or three people who had been staring into the
coffin moved aside to let me see. I looked over the edge
of the coffin into the calm white face of an old woman.

Somebody touched me as I turned away and left the
room. I felt a thread of laughter in my throat as I went
down the stairs, and there, at the bottom, was the old
man. He lifted his benign face to me. " Are ye goin'
on ? " he asked softly. He drew my hand between his

own. "We wur married near sixty years" he said,
nodding to me and smiling. I withdrew my hand
gently and left him there, smiling at the wall.

"Do you know if there's another funeral in the
street ?" I asked a small boy at the door. He turned
and shouted my question to a woman leaning in a doorway. She unfolded her bare arms and jerked a thumb.
"They're buryin' a wee girl away up at the Crumlin
Road end. About a hundred-an'-fifty-somethin'. Ye'll
see the hearse."

When I got to the house of the dead girl, people were
coming out of the doorway, and gathering in the street.
I recognised Bob immediately. We shook hands and
murmured a few words. I saw the boy. He stood with
a brown hat drooping from his square oil-stained fingers.
A cornerboy, he had taken on overnight, the dignity of a
man. He had a lonely look. In a short time the last
sign of anything which bound him to these strangers
would be hidden. The kisses, the quarrels, the hot
whisperings would not take on the grace of memory. He
was too young for that. In a week he would be spending
his experience in another doorway, in another street.

At an upper window a woman appeared, pressing her
hand to her mouth. Then someone drew her away. As
we moved slowly down the street, blinds were drawn in
the houses. Slowly the carriages and file of men drew
over to the left. A funeral was coming up the street. I
could see the old man trudging behind the hearse, his
eyes fixed on the ever-rising rim. As we came closer,
the man with the football medal saw me. For an
instant I saw his hand rise in recognition. I gazed
through his face as if it had been glass. With funereal
steps we approached, passed, and drew apart.

THE BROKEN TREE

HANS eased the clear colter of the plough on to the rig and swung the horse to the downward furrow. As the rhythmic throb of the car engine dropped, and then beat swiftly towards him, he checked the horse, and watched the car's roof rushing above the hedges towards the farm house. Horse, metal and man stood motionless until the car disappeared behind the gable and the sound of its engine stopped. "Hup, Darkie" said the man, slapping the horse's flank with a rein. He inserted the colter again, and the earth curled back from the gleaming share.

He was halfway on the upward furrow when he heard the gulls that had been gleaning at his heels, cry and wheel away over his shoulder. His brother-in-law was coming up the unploughed land after him. As he overtook Hans he moved his head sidewards in greeting. Hans took a fresh grip on reins and plough handle. "How are ye, William" he said. In silence, the horse, the plough and the two men moved to the head of the field.

As the horse wheeled to the untilled strip, William crossed over to Hans' left side. "Are ye quitting soon ?" he asked. Hans raised his face to the brittle evening sky. "I'm quittin' at the head o' this yin" he answered. As Hans unhooked the traces, William pushed his hands behind his coat tails. "Aggie an' me just tuk a run down in the car" he said. "I thought I

heard ye on the loanen " answered Hans, straightening
up and throwing the swingle tree on his shoulder. He
caught Darkie's bridle, and William hurried on to open
the gate.

When they came to the first house in the loanen, Hans
stepped to the half-door. He nodded to William, " Have
a luk at that " he said. William looked over the door
and saw a small red cow. There was a musical run from
her chain as she turned to look at the two. " Stan'
there " said Hans to the horse, and pushed the byre door
open. As they edged up beside her the cow raised her
head, her large limpid eye turned back on them. " She's
a nice beast." said William. Hans slid his hand down
the cow's neck. " She's a wee lady." he said.

As they walked up the loanen, Hans leaned over
Darkie's drooping head. " I had her tae to the bull, an'
I'm goin' tae hae a cow calf." he said. William laughed.
" How d'ye know it'll be a cow calf, man ? " Hans
smiled and nodded. " I'm goin' tae hae a wee heefer."
he said.

They were near the farm when William asked " Did
she cost ye much ? " There was a pause. " Twenty
poun' " answered Hans. " It's a risk." said William
sagely. Suddenly he stopped at a gate, hooking his heel
on the bottom bar. " Hans " he said urgently, " Hans,
before we go in." Hans stopped and the horse sidled
in the narrow lane, leaning his head over his master's
shoulder. " What is it, William ? " asked Hans, running
his fingers up Darkie's jaw. " How would ye like a job
in town ? I'm drainin' off slobland for an aerodrome,
an' I could give ye a start as a ganger. What d'ye
say ? " " I told ye before. I wont hear tell av it !

I've a farm an' I'm workin' it. I know damn fine
Maisie's been at Aggie. William, don't ask me again.
Your work's buildin' ; my work's farmin'." He stepped
forward, pulling sharply at Darkie's mouth. As they
walked, the slow clip clop of the hooves calmed him.
" Thanks all the same, William," he said as they paused
at the farm-close gate. He led Darkie to the stable and
William went into the house. When he had tended to
the horse he washed his hands at the butt and stood for a
moment looking down over the fields. The sinking sun
laid a cold bright finger on the ploughed land. The
furrows gleamed on the hill like fresh combed hair.

As he crossed the close he saw two or three feathers
clinging to the chopping block. He smiled as he thought
of Maisie playing Lady Bountiful to her sister. When
he entered the kitchen William's wife rose from her
chair and lowered the kettle on the crane. " Hello,
Hans." she said cheerfully. Hans nodded and smiled,
" How are ye, Aggie." he said. As he went to his chair
at the head of the table, his wife raised her flushed pretty
face from the fire. She balanced the caddy spoon over
the teapot. " Are ye ready ? " she asked briefly. " I'm
ready," said Hans planting his elbows on each side of his
plate.

After the meal Aggie and William wouldn't sit down
again. The children, they said, would be waiting on
them. Hans brought a hurricane lamp and lighted
them to the car. He saw the fowl, ill wrapped in paper,
lying on the back seat. The engine whirred and
throbbed into life. The car moved forward, Aggie
turning round to wave, William peering ahead into the
dark, one hand raised from the steering wheel in farewell.

" I'm goin' round the houses," said Hans, when they had gone. " I'll be back in a minute." He stood for a long time gazing into the byre. " How are ye, lady ? " he whispered into the warm darkness. There was a soft low and a ripple of the polished chain. With a smile on his lips he closed the top half-door and went home.

Maisie had washed up when he got back. She sat darning at the hearth. He lifted down a fresh pipe from the mantelpiece. " Aggie lukked bravely." he said as he turned his blade in the bowl. " She did," answered his wife. He leaned forward to knock his pipe out on the firebars, and spoke again. " Maisie," he said " don't get at Aggie again to get a job for me in town." She let her darning fall, her eyes fixed on his dark head still bent over the hearth. He raised his face and she saw that he was smiling. " Well, what if I did ask her ! " she burst out, " I'm tired av livin' in all this clabber an' mud. I want to go an' live in the town. I want a house like Aggie's ! " " You wouldn't have a house like Aggie's," he answered gently. " William owns the place he works in. I wud only be a kind av head labourer . . . . ." " An' what are ye here. Ye've only rented yer great farm from oul Aspinall. We'll never pay it off ! " " It'll be paid off " he said " an' it'll be ours. To work fur William means livin' in a brick box in some street. Ye know what that means . . . ."

She sprang to her feet, her scissors jangling on the floor. " Ye would cast that up ! " she shouted, " I knew you'd cast that up on me . . . . ." Hans stood up and put his hands in his pockets. " I'm casting nothin' up, darlin'. Yer the dearest wife a man cud have." He

moved to the door, opened it, and leaned against the
doorpost.   He looked out, not across the dark fields, but
at the great starry roof above him.   His eyes caught and
settled on the lights of the big house on the hill.   I'll
have to gather up the quarter's rent next week, he
thought.   Behind him, Maisie searched aimlessly on the
floor for her scissors, then she put the sock to her mouth
and snapped the wool in her teeth.   Suddenly, with a
sob she threw down the work and rushed to the inner
door.   Hans overtook her in quick strides.   In the dark
hall he took the weeping girl in his arms.   She stood with
head down, her fists braced against his chest.   Suddenly
she gave in to the gentle insistent pull of his arms so
that he staggered.   She caught him by the shoulders
pressing her mouth against his until his lips hurt.   He
picked her up and carried her back to the firelit kitchen.

Spring came, warm and turbulent.   Hans had the
corn sown when William visited them again.   He came
alone, greeting them with a wave as he clambered out of
the car.   " Aha," he cried when he saw Maisie draining
a pot of potatoes in the runlet, " I thought I wudn't be in
time, but I kept my foot down all the way from town—
and lived in hope ! "   " Yer in time, alright, William "
answered Hans, laughing.   " D'ye want tae wash yer
hands afore ye sit down ? "   " I know my way " said
William crossing to the inner door.   They heard him in
the dairy, dipping water from the crock, and the soft
squattering of him soaping his hands.   Their glances
met and then William blundered into the kitchen, his
eyes screwed tight, his dripping hands groping blindly.
With a laugh, Maisie whipped a towel from the line and
caught his head in it.

"Well, I've got my dinner, an' ye can hunt me when ye like" said William pushing his cup away. "But I'm down to stay fur a coupl' a days, if ye'll have me." He had brought them news of the city and of their relatives, imparting that joy of the visitor which is now only experienced in lonely countrysides. Maisie cried out in pleasure "Can ye stay, William! Oh, why didn't ye bring Aggie?" "She's away at her Aunt Beth's fur two days" he answered shortly. "Well, Hans," he added, "Will ye give me an' oul pair av breeks an' I'll hag wood for ye?" "I'll let ye roll the knowe field if ye think ye can handle Darkie" said Hans. "Good, good—get me the breeks an' show me my work." Hans rose, "Come on, William" he said, "if yer ready."

During the two days William rolled in the corn, helped Hans clean the linthole and took the springcart to Newtowndullard for meal. Hans showed him the cow again. She was well gone in calf, round in the belly and languorous. She moved slowly in the field setting down her pointed hooves delicately. William praised her, and when he went to fetch her in the evenings he urged her slowly, flicking her with a thin privet twig. When he drove away on the third day, Hans came forward to the car and shook him by the hand. They parted good friends.

In the early summer the farm gathered itself in response to the labour of Hans and Maisie. The girl went about her work gladly now, and the sullenness of the winter seemed to have gone. Under her care four broods of chickens piped through the close, and when the ceiling lamp was lighted, she sat with her flowering hoops stitching lovely needle work on linen for a few pence a piece. In the evenings she went for the cow, leaning over the gate to cry *chay*, *chay*, *chay*, and watching with understanding eyes the slow careful steps of the beast as it came at her bidding. The corn was rising round the knowe, pale green and strong, and by July a white shock of hay stood in the field at the house gable.

Hans borrowed a reaper from Lady Aspinall's steward to cut the hay. Shuey Murray and his son were binding behind Hans, and at noon Maisie brought tea and farls and boiled eggs out to the field, and stayed to bind, for the Murray boy had slipped away across the fields, tired of the heat and the prickly seeds in his shirt. Hans was settled back in the seat of the reaper as it whirred down the long sward, lazy in the heat. A green frog sprang over the flickering knife. Faintly, across the fields, he heard his name *Hans*! *Hi, Hans*! "Hans," Maisie called, "Somebody's shoutin' on ye." The three people stopped to watch the boy rushing down the slope above them. His waving arms and staring face were pregnant with disaster. He burst through the hedge and stumbled forward, his knees knocking together with fatigue. "Hans, Hans, yer wee coo's cowped in the sheugh!" The man bounded clear from the reaper and grasped the boy's arm. "Where is she? What made her fa'?" He gulped and pointed over the hill. "She's lyin' tither side on her back—a swelled up wi' clover." Hans was running across the field to the house. At the gate he turned and shouted "Shuey, send the wean fur a rope, an' fetch Paddy McCarey an' his knife!" The boy sped from his father's grasp and Shuey hurried across the field to McCarey's.

The cow was lying on her back in a deep ditch. As they approached she coughed convulsively and her muzzle furred with froth. Three men were already there, and were trying to turn her and pull her from the ditch by her legs and neck. One of them eased himself up and spat. " She'll no dae it, Hans," he said, " an' we dinna want tae hurt the calf. If we cud get a rope an' pulley ower that bush we cud ease her up." A lad stepped forward, and pulling off his jacket, caught the slim sapling and shook it. " It might houl," he said, and climbed several feet into its branches. " Throw me the rope," he cried and stretched down his hand.

As he was rigging the pulley, Shuey Murray and Paddy McCarey came down the field. McCarey, an old man, glanced at the cow, then nodded silently to the others, his mouth gaping for breath. He bent down quickly and slid the knife into the hide, piercing the wall of the first stomach. There was a sudden whistling sound from between his hands, and the men bending over his shoulder drew back quickly as the foul gas caught their nostrils. The rope smacked down among them as the young man in the tree leaned out and ran it through the block. Then he came sliding down the tree. " Under her shoulders an' rump " he said, springing over the animal. They worked the ropes under her, and men caught the running ends and started to pull, backing across the field. Slowly the cow came up out of the ditch, and as hands stretched out to swing her on to the grass the tree screamed, slivered down, and broke. For a moment the gross body hung arched in the air, then fell, the neck striking a ridge in the sheugh face. The animal gave a long bubbling sigh, her legs and body stretched in a convulsion of agony, and the dung ran out over her tail.

The men stepped back in silence, lifting their coats and rolling down their sleeves. The young man who had climbed the tree went over and put his hand on the muzzle of the dead beast. He sprang over her and grasped the shattered pillar of the sapling, looking up into the green chaos. " A bloody sycamore for all the world ! " he said.

Hans stood apart, staring with dull eyes at the cow. Paddy McCarey picked up his coat and came over to him, shaking his head. Shuey Murray called to his son, " Away up to the house an' bring a couple o' spades." McCarey had got into his coat. " Houl on Shuey " he said. He turned to Hans. " Yer no' goin' tae bury that guid beef, Hans man ? Tak a leg aff her fur yerself. Send the wean up tae the hoose fur a knife an' a hacksaw." Hans started violently. " No, no," he said, turning away abruptly. " Weel, damn it, dae ye mind if I tak a piece aff her ? " ' An' me, Hans ? " the Man from the Lough asked. " Tak what ye want," said Hans slowly. The boy returned with the knife and spades. As McCarey caught the hind leg between his thighs and began to slit the hide, Hans turned away and climbed the hill, Maisie by his side. At the top he turned and looked down at the cluster of men. Someone gave a distant shout of laughter and started to walk away. It was the Man from the Lough with a leg of meat over his shoulder. Two men were stooped, digging, and on her broken back lay the cow, the four stumps of her legs turned to the sky.

They went back to the house, and when Maisie was

halfway across the kitchen floor her legs gave way and
she fell weeping on the sofa.

Hans stood over her stupidly. At last he touched her
shoulder, " Don't cry, girl," he said, " don't cry."
" Damn ye, give over, Maisie, will ye ! " he shouted.
He turned to the window and then he heard the soft
noise of her as she slid to the floor. She half lay, half
knelt on the tiles, her knuckles shining white on the sofa
cover. Dimly he realised her passionate distress. He
crossed the kitchen and knelt beside her. " Maisie " he
whispered hoarsely, " Maisie, is it yerself now ? "   He
felt the gentle pressure of her head against his cheek.
He put his arms around her and laid his face in her lap.
After a time he got up and went out to the corner of the
house, over the half mown field. Something older than
time filled him. Maisie and her child would live, the
cow and its calf were dead. He shivered and drew
himself up, clasping the house corner with his hand.
" The Lord giveth, and the Lord taketh away " he said
aloud. The soft evening wind came to him over the
aching stubble of the field.

The hay was mown. Hans and his wife moved
steadily day by day through the labour of the farm ;
fencing, gleaning, searching every crevice through which
the farm's wealth might seep out. On the third evening
Maisie took a rod from the hearth cheek. " I'm away
for Lady." she said, drawing a shawl over her head.
They stood looking at each other, and then Hans
laughed and caught her in his arms. He took the rod
from her hand and laid it in the corner. The coming
of the child seemed to have rid the death of the cow from
both their minds. Dimly Hans connected the child and

the loss of his animals. But he thrust it away. Four
months, he would say, and I'll have the potatoes and
corn in. Maisie saw more clearly. She would not bear
her child in the rough sunny room at the end of the
house. Already she knew the cost of a confinement in
Newtowndullard Hospital. This alone would drive her
out in a raw dawn to tend a gaping chick or search for an
afternoon in nettle thickets for hens that laid away.

Three weeks later, when Hans was working in the
close, a constable came round the end of the house,
wheeling a bicycle. He was a dull redfaced man with a
dispatch case on his back. He crossed over to Hans and
leaned the bicycle against his thigh. " There's powerful
bloody thorns in yer loanen." he said, jerking his head
back. Hans squatting with a nail in his mouth, nodded
shortly. " Y'er Mr. Hans Gault ? " asked the constable,
fumbling at his case. Hans stood up, " Aye," he said,
" Gault." The constable took out a long folded paper
and handed it to him. " Whut's this ? " asked Hans,
opening it. The constable nodded at the paper as Hans
spread it out. " . . . . . did unlawfully dispose of a
carcase of meat to persons named, and in acting accordingly did commit an offence under Emergency (Abattoir
Regulations) Ch. V. Act . . . . . the said Defendant is
summoned to appear . . . . . to answer charges stated
above." " Whut charges ? " The constable had swung
his bicycle round but at Hans' question he took the
paper and ran his eye over it. " Three charges " he
said, " Wan, Ministry av Health, *tuberculosis*; two,
rationin' av meat; three, cruelty t' animals. The beast,
it would seem, wusn't slaughtered humanely." " But,

god, I didn't slaughter her at all. She broke her back in a sheugh."   " Did ye report it ? "   The constable threw his leg over the bicycle and balanced on his square black toe.   " Ah, ye see, there ye are.   Ye shud always report things like that, now there's a war on. Well, it wus a poor errand, but peelers cant be choosers."   His grin faded.   " Well, good-day to you."   At the corner he turned, wobbling.   " Did I remark on the thorns in the loanen ? "   Hans stood staring after him silently.   " Ye cud pick up a pumpture right an' easy."   The bicycle carried him round the corner and out of sight.

She sat silent after he had finished, looking now at the summons where he had tossed it on the table, now at her husband as he sat over the fire.   She was troubled and confused ; afraid because of his collapse, yearning because of his trouble, unable to stifle the hope that this meant leaving the farm.   Hans jumped up, kicking the chair away, and strode to the window.   He grasped the sill in his powerful hands.   " God damn me " he said, " if ever I give onythin' away again."   " What are ye goin' to do ? " she asked.   He turned, buttoning his shirt.   " I'll go over to Newtowndullard an' see O'Brien. I'll get advice."

The fat dusty solicitor could do little for him.   He tried every way to cajole his Worship but Hans was found guilty on two counts and fined twenty pounds on each.   The charge of cruelty was withdrawn.

They sat together in the kitchen one evening about a week later.   Hans had cycled back from Newtown-dullard fifty pounds poorer.   Suddenly he turned to her and spoke in a slow deliberate voice, " Well, ye'll be content now. This means the end o' us. Ye'll get livin' in town after all." The girl stiffened in pain and anger. Since their trouble she had crushed down every thought of herself. Now Hans in his blundering cruelty had freed her. " I am glad ! I am ! Now mebbe I can have my baby somewhere than an oul limed backroom !" Rushing into her mind came the thought that he had spent so much time talking and brooding over the calf and had discovered the coming of his child by accident. She rose, her face bright with anger. " I hate ye, Hans Gault ! I hate ye ! " With her hand to her mouth she ran from the room. She paused in the hall. She heard him rise, heard him fumbling for his cap, the clack of the door and his long light stride round the end of the house. Hours later she heard him creep like a cat over the kitchen floor, the drunken stumble in the hall, and felt him fumble his way to bed. She lay, breathing slowly and gently, as if asleep.

A letter came from Aggie. She had found an un-furnished house for them. Maisie went up by bus and next day a lorry piled with their furniture moved out of the close, Hans sitting beside the driver. That evening they worked together in the tiny angular house arranging the furniture.

William and Aggie called at supper-time. Aggie was full of excuses for not being able to help. After they had a cup of tea William moved over beside Hans. " Y'er well fixed up here " he said. Hans took the pipe from his mouth, " It'll do " he replied, " I havna seen the back yet." " Oh, there's a wee garden beyond the yard." said Aggie eagerly. There was a silence broken

only by the puffing of Hans as he stared at the new fire.
" I might be able to get ye a job, Hans," said William
at last. " Might . . . . . " the word burst from
Maisie. Their eyes met. William spoke with difficulty
" Ye see " he said, " the contract's not goin' well. I've
had to lay off a lot av men. But I could give ye a job as
a watchman. It wud keep ye goin' till things brisked
up. What do ye say ? " Hans looked across at his
wife but she had lowered her head and was running her
finger slowly up and down her skirt. Hans rose.
" Thanks, William," he said, " I'll tak it till something
better turns up." William almost jumped in relief to
grasp Hans' hand. " Don't worry," he said, " I'll look
after ye, Hans boy."

Maisie was happy in their new home. In the morn-
ings Hans would lie, listening drowsily to her and the
woman next door conversing in the back, their mouths
full of clothes pegs. Sometimes she would stand in the
late afternoon sun and talk to her neighbours over the
street gate. At four she would hurry indoors to make
Hans his tea and parcel up his supper.

Hans slept at night in a hut beside a yard filled with
concrete mixers, picks and shovels. Early in the morning he would be roused by six old men coming in, one
by one, and sitting in a row opposite him. They were
road-sweepers, decrepit creatures too old to labour.
When he got up and went out to turn down his lamps
they started to whisper to each other. They fell silent
when he came back, and sat hands on knees, gazing
shyly into the fire. Micky Conn was always the first to
arrive. He was an old man, morbidly clean, who had
lost an eye at Spion Kop. He told long wandering

stories of his own and his comrades' gallantry, of the invincibility of Irishmen in battle.

The weekends were the hardest on him. From noon on Saturday until Sunday evening he stayed in the hut gazing into the fire or wandering aimlessly round the yard. From the hut door he had a vista across the city to the checkered hills which rose above the valley. Hungrily he watched the seasons through the frame of gaunt walls. He knew how it was with the fields, whether they lay asleep and rustling drenched in the white sunlight, or trampled by the pillars of rain which strode along the hills . . . . .

The voice kept shouting, *Hans ! Hi, Hans . .* He sat up on the bench, shaking his head and blinking his eyes. A policeman stood in the door, rain streaming from his cap and coat. " Your lamps are blown over " he said, " you'd better come out an' have a look at them." He pulled on a coat and followed the policeman. The lamps were out except one which lay on its side, the flame spurting wildly in the wind. It shone on the long slim heads of the picks, and drew a line of crimson down the shafts, polished by the hands of labouring men. He set the lamp upright again, and went round the yard, lighting the others, one by one.

THURSDAY NIGHTS

EVERY movement she made was dramatised from the moment she replaced the 'phone in its cradle. She became aware of her curling pink fingers, of her legs caught in the long skirt of the formal black dress which all Messrs. Hamiltons' young ladies wore. She arched her ankles and lifted her head as she passed under the sullen stare of Mr. O'Connor, the shopwalker. As she approached the fancies the three other girls leaned forward on the glass-topped counter, supporting themselves on their fingers (they all wore engagement rings, and one was really engaged), " Well, well ? " they whispered eagerly. Maureen turned in behind the counter and busied herself with a tangle of ribbons. " Well, what ? " she asked, trying to keep her voice even, and a smile of pride from her mouth. " No foolin, Croskery ! " said one (the really engaged one) " was it the officer fella ? "

Maureen turned a beaming face on them. " Yes, he 'phoned. He said at the dance he'd 'phone. I'm going out with him to-night."

At five minutes to six a bell trills among all the departments on all the three floors of Messrs. Hamiltons. Young ladies with black bags under their arms, and young men with surreptitious cigarettes in their palms, dash from behind counters, up stairs into cloakrooms. A narrow side entrance beside the time-clock is open to allow the staff to depart. Here, slim young ladies in elegant costumes punch time-cards, and go out to meet their steadies.

On the opposite pavement, the steadies stand in a row. Some have been there so long, they know other steadies to speak to, and have a drink with now and again. Some steadies stand with their eyes on the gate waiting for a beloved hat or familiar shoulder. Others, (the older ones) stand talking, waiting for their sleeves to be plucked. Hullo, I'm here. They move off amid a general flicking of hatbrims.

He crossed the street, " Hullo, Maureen," he said, smiling down uncertainly, for he felt things were going wrong. " Oh, hullo, Jimmie," she answered, with a bright smile. " We'll have our tea at the Rialto," he said, falling into step with her, " and I'll get the tickets afterwards." It'll keep, she said to herself, I'll tell him at tea. They entered the café, as Belfast lovers do, Jimmie striding ahead, looking for a vacant table, leaving Maureen to pull out her chair when they had secured one.

" I can't go to the pictures to-night, Jimmie," she said. He laid down his fork and stared at her. He hadn't taken off his overcoat, she noticed with irritation. " But, what—what do you mean, Maureen ; you can't go to the pictures ? "

" I'm sorry, Jimmie. I—I forgot I had to go out to-night."

" But this is Thursday. This is our night. This is the night we always go out. You couldn't have anything to do on a Thursday night ! "

Her voice had suddenly gone hard. " What makes

you so sure ?   I've somewhere to go *this* Thursday night."

He sat silent for a little time.   " Maureen," he said, " tell me, is it another fella ? "

" Yes."

He lowered his head and moved it slowly from side to side, like a young animal heavily struck.   " Are ye goin' with this fella ? "

" Mebbe.   I might be."

" I suppose you want me to clear off then, Maureen ? "

" Oh, Jimmie, I do like you, reely.   But I don't love you.   Somehow, we don't seem to have anything in common now."

" D'you want me to go, Maureen ? "

" Oh, don't go on saying that, Jimmie ! It's just that we don't seem to get as much fun out of things together, now.   Jimmie dear, don't let it hurt you, please ! "

He beckoned to the waitress and rose heavily.   " I suppose we'd better be goin' ! Your gloves are lying on thon chair."

They left the cinema café and walked through the streets in silence, side by side, to Donegall Place. Jimmie stood on the edge of the pavement staring at the traffic.   " There's no hope for me then, Maureen," he said, without turning his head.

" I'm terribly sorry, Jimmie.   Please don't let it hurt you."

" For Christ's sake stop talking about it hurting me ! " he swung round on her, his face hard with anger.   Then his eyes filled with pain and fear again.   " Goodbye, Maureen kid," he shook her shoulder tenderly, " I hope things go well with you."   He gazed into her face for a second, then, turning, moved into the rushing crowd. Maureen failed to hear the cheery salute of the officer who had crossed the pavement. " I said ' I wondered when you were getting rid of the boy friend.' "

" Oh—oh, hullo ! He wasn't reely a boy friend, just a boy I know, waiting for a tram."

" And he gave it up and decided to walk, wise man. Well, where would you like to go from here ? "

" I thought, perhaps, we could go to the Rialto."

" Oh, its a rotten film, you know. One of those American success stories. Girl's in love with a man and sets out to convince him she's not—and succeeds."

" Why ? Oh, well, it doesn't matter. Have you any ideas ? "

" I thought we might go dancing at the Khaki Klub."

" But I was dancing last night," Maureen demurred.

" This is just a hop, and I promise you'll get the last bus home."

" Well—alright."

" Splendid ! And now for a drink."

" But I — do you really want one ? "

" Rather ! and so do you." He took her arm and together they crossed the wide Place to the Queen Café. When they were seated he leaned over smiling, " You'd like — ? " " A little sherry, please."

" Dry ? A dry sherry and a rye and dry," he called to the barmaid.

He sipped his whisky slowly, smiling at her over his glass. Maureen's eyes ranged the bottles, then she lowered them to smile in reply. He'll want another she thought, something fancy. She studied the names on the bottles, outlandish words. Benedictine, that was easy.

" Let's have another, then we'll go."

" Alright. I'll have—Benedictine." She took a florin from her purse. " Please let me pay for this one."

He laughed, catching her hand, " Of course I won't. As a matter of fact I'm celebrating our victory at Balaklava."

" Oh." Maureen put the coin back in her purse. " I didn't hear the six o'clock news, to-night," she said.

The Khaki Klub is a social club for officers and their lady friends, pensive beautiful creatures with smiles rouged on their faces, and a distressing nervous habit of crossing their legs well above the knee when they sit down. The appearance of a healthy pretty girl who was a superb dancer caused a thrill of excitement and apprehension to pass through the occupants of the side tables. Soon, the vapid masks knew, subtle strategy would be employed for a temporary withdrawal.

Maureen danced with jovial colonels, with handsome majors, much to Lieutenant Peter Newman's chagrin, and once was carried round the floor on a major-general's stomach. Then Peter and she had coffee and sandwiches and cigarettes. " Enjoy it ? " he asked as they drifted through the last dim-lighted waltz. " Thank you, I did. I enjoyed every minute of it."

Of course they missed the last bus and had to take a taxi. In the taxi Peter took her in his arms and kissed her. " Let us go again, soon " he whispered to the pale face on his shoulder. " I'd love to — soon. 'Phone me,

won't you ? "   As she spoke the taxi jerked to a stand-still.   " This is my house.   No, please don't get out.
My mother will be waiting, I'm sure.   Good night,
Peter dear, thanks awfully."

" But look here," he leaned eagerly from the taxi
window.   " Can't we be more definite ?   How about
this night week ? "

" Oh, no, not Thursday.   I'm booked every Thurs-day.   Give me a 'phone soon.   There — good night and
thanks again."

A FISH WITHOUT CHIPS.

" Who's the tall doll ?"

" What'n ?"

Davie drew the end of a chip into his mouth and glanced across at the opposite box. " Huh, that'n," he said. " That's my sister. She's a pain in the neck, that dame."

" She may be a pain in the neck to you " hummed Charlie " but she's a bit of all right to me."

" I'm tellin' ye, mate," said Davie, chasing a fragment through the vinegar. " I live in the same house."

Charlie leaned back, watching from the end of his eye the four girls in the opposite box. The girl in the blue coat talked vivaciously to her companions, helping her story with expressive hands. As she raised her head she shot oblique glances at the boys. When at last her friends blossomed into laughter, she leaned back with a smile of triumph. As the boys pushed back their plates and buttoned their coats, the girls rose suddenly and left the saloon. Davie grinned pleasantly as his sister passed. " Hullo, Sis," he said.

As they walked homewards they talked of Glentoran's chances in the Gold Cup. Suddenly, when they reached the street corner where they parted, Charlie said " Does she go with a fella ?" Davie was lost for a moment. " Oh, you mean Sis ? No, she wus goin' with a fella, but she knocked off because he was always complainin' about pimples on his neck. She told our oul' lady she didn't mind him havin' pimples, but he didn't need to show off about it. That's the way she gets on." Charlie shrugged his collar round his smooth young neck. " Hi, Davie, how about puttin' on a date fur us ?"

" Naw, I will not," laughed Davie, " I owe ye no grudge."

" Come on, come on," urged Charlie impatiently, " no foolin' Davie—put on a date fur a fella."

" Ah, do yer own dirty work," answered Davie, moving away from his mate's hand. " Sure ye'll see her around the place before long."

" I've never seen her before, an' ye know it.   Are ye gonna put on a date fur us ?"

" Well, why don't ye do it yerself ?"

" Sure I don't know the dame to speak to !"

Davie stared at his mate in surprise.   " That's the first time I ever knew that *you* had to know a doll to speak to, before ye spoke to her !"

" This is different " answered Charlie.   " She's your sister " he added maliciously.

" She's got to take her chance wi' the rest" said Davie.

" I tell ye what," said Charlie, holding the other's lapel, " if ye won't put on a date fur us, will ye tell her I wus askin' fur her ?"

" Oh, anythin' fur a quiet life !" cried Davie.

" O.K., Davie, I'll be seein' ye."

" I'll be seein' ye." returned Davie, with a half salute, and they parted at the corner.

The two boys worked as apprentices in the same turning-shop under Big Archie Glass, the leading hand, whose skin, teeth and hair were of a uniform fawn shade, and whose mind was as dingy as his teeth.   Big Archie,

with his starved body and prurient mind, had early come
to strife with the boys. After a time, the healthy and
more stable Davie came to regard his boss with contempt,
but he remained a thing of fascination and hatred to
Charlie, who, slowly and unknowingly, grew to idealise
that which Big Archie befouled.

" Well, what'd she say ? "asked Charlie the next
morning. " I never seen her " answered Davie, " she
wus in bed when I got back." " Ye'll see her to-night,
won't ye ?" " I might " answered Davie with a nod.

The following day, Davie's reply was the same, and
Charlie refrained from asking him again. A feeling of
restraint grew between the boys. It was Davie who
came up at lunch-hour some days later, and set his tea-
can down beside Charlie's. " I told Sis about that."
he said. Charlie looked up suspiciously, "Well, what'd
she say ?" " She sends it back." Davie stopped.
" An' what the hell does that mean ?" demanded
Charlie in exasperation. " Oh, I dunno," said Davie
with a shrug, " I suppose she means she's askin' fur ye."

Charlie drew back, abashed. " Oh — thanks, Davie.
Well, tell her I wus askin' fur her, an' will she go out
some night ?" He drained his can, arose, and joined
some men quoiting at the end of the shop.

Aware now that he could move the reluctant Davie,
Charlie avoided his friend after working-hours. They
met by chance at the Oval, where, pressed together in
a bank of Glentoran supporters, they gave themselves
up to the partisan rhythm.

" Sis'll see ye on Thursday night," said Davie suddenly, as the half-time whistle sounded, and the crowd
broke into thousands of opinionated men.

" O.K., Davie," said Charlie with a friendly smile,
" where ?"

" At the Belmont, at sivin."

" Did she say Thursday, herself ?"

" Uh-huh. It's the only night she has free."

Charlie felt a twinge of jealousy. " It's not a very
good night," he said, " just before pay-day."

" Take her a walk up the hills." said Davie, with
studied friendliness.

" There's dames ye can't take a walk the first night.
Anyway, tell her Thursday night's O.K."

The affair now leaped forward in Charlie's mind. It
obtruded in his thoughts, and his actions, at home and at
work, became self-conscious and self-criticised. One
evening he went to the Municipal College for a syllabus
of the Machine Drawing and Shop Practice night classes.
When he walked down Newtownards Road, he greeted
his workmates with restraint and dignity. Next week
they would be saying " Dy'e see that fella there. He
goes with a fine jane."

Was she a fine jane ? In his brooding over her, he
could not now recall her face, as though in filling in the
background, he had smudged the head. He remembered with delight the undeniable impression she had
made on him in the supper saloon. But he wore them
smooth with remembering ; the curved eloquent finger,
the head caught in laughter.

He moved near to Davie as they crossed Fraser Street
bridge on their way home. " Could ye get me a phota
av yer sister ? " he asked. Davie turned to him in surprise. " For Jasus's sake !" he exclaimed with laughter,
Charlie drew away, red with anger.

By denying himself the pictures and cigarettes, he saved four shillings which he put in the breast pocket of his boiler suit, before he set out to work on Thursday. He fidgeted, and shirked the little jobs at the bench all the morning, moving off on errands at the slightest excuse. He was full of excitement and apprehension, his mind wavering at the magnetic hour of seven.

At lunch-time as he quoited, the money fell from his pocket, and Big Archie slapped down the rolling coins with the boots. He picked them up and bit them before he handed them to Charlie. " B'god, they're real ! " he cried.

In the afternoon Charlie had to make a new rod for a feed pump, and Big Archie watched him with angry impatience, as he fumbled with the lathe. " What the hell's houldin' ye ! " he cried at last. " Lend me yer calipers, will ye ? " asked Charlie, " I've lost mine." " Here." The boss tossed him over the tool. " An' get a move on, will ye ? " He blundered through the job, and when running the saddle up to put in a parting-tool, caught the calipers in the whirling chuck of the lathe and smashed them. He groped for the broken tool and tossed it on to the bench.

A few minutes before knocking-off time, Big Archie leaned over the bench. " Gimme the calipers," he said. Charlie rummaged on the bench and held out the twisted metal to the man. " They're bust, Archie," he said. Big Archie looked at the tool, his mouth opening in feigned consternation. " Well, b'god, you're a cool boyo." He mimicked the boy: " *They're bust, Archie.*" His voice rose suddenly in anger. " What the hell sort av a cratur are ye ? D'ye know those cost me four

bob ? "   " I'll get a bit av steel an' turn ye off a pair "
said Charlie.   " Ye'll do damn all av the sort ! " shouted
the man, ye'll pay me four bob for the pair ye bust ! "

" Ye'll get yer four bob, all right ! " shouted Charlie,
then his voice dropped in fear as Big Archie opened his
hand, " The morra," he added.

" No, now," said Big Archie softly, jerking his thumb
at Charlie's breast pocket.   " Ye have it on ye."

" It'll do as well the morra " replied Charlie, turning
his back on the man.   Big Archie slid his hand over
Charlie's shoulder, and grasping the throat of his shirt,
turned him against the wall.   " Gimme the money " he
said menacingly, his body arched away from Charlie's
feet.   With a choking cry, Charlie tore away the hand at
his throat, and in one movement threw his opponent
back and hurled the money at him.   " There ye are, ye
pig ye ! " he cried, and darting under the man's arm he
ran out of the workshop.   Suddenly he stopped, cursing
himself for a cowardly fool.   He wouldn't let Big
Archie get away with it, even if he had to bat him with a
spanner.   He ran back through the streaming men.
The workshop was deserted, Archie was gone.

When he had finished his dinner, he sat spelling the
upside-down print of the newspaper on the table.
" Ma," he said to the woman at the range, " have ye any
money ? "   " Tons av it." she replied, without turning,
" ye'll get it when I die."   " Could ye lend me four
bob ? "   His mother paused in replacing the tea-caddy
on the mantelpiece, and looked at him for a long second,
silently.   The boy kicked his chair back angrily, and
went upstairs.

He pulled his Sunday trousers out from under the

mattress, noting their sharp creases with sombre satisfaction. We could go for a walk, he thought, if it doesn't rain. A humid little wind puffed at the curtains. He dressed with particular care, a clean shirt and clean socks, and took his blue tie out of the family Bible. As he passed the kitchen door his mother called on him, where was he going. Out, he said, and pulled the door on her angry voice. As the door closed the pavement was suddenly freckled with rain.

He left the tram opposite the Belmont and stood in a deep doorway, sheltered from the bouncing rain. Trams pulled up at the Cinema and people scurried over the gleaming pavement, in under the canopy. The chromium doors were never still, swinging and shutting, and inside he could see elegant persons moving amongst the palms in the foyer. Then he saw her ; clicking over the pavement, shaking her umbrella. Slender and lovely, she stood silhouetted against the pastel light. Charlie ground his hands in his pocket linings. For minutes they stood, thirty paces apart, waiting for each other. Now she had ceased to watch the emptying trams. She opened and shut her umbrella angrily. At seven minutes past seven she gave a last disdainful look up and down the street, then running across the pavement, boarded a tram. As she disappeared into the lower cabin Charlie took a convulsive step forward. He stood motionless on the streaming road until the tram had vanished into the rain.

He was at work early the next morning. After he had hung up his cap and jacket he turned to find Davie standing close behind him. They stared at each other for a moment. " Hello, Davie," he said, " I had a bit

av bad . . . . ." Davie's face was hard as he thrust
it forward. " Shut it," he said. " You've a brass
neck, talking to me, lettin' my sister down an' makin' a
cod outa me ; ye blirt ye."

As Charlie opened his mouth, Davie struck him on
the face with a clod of waste.   He sent him further back
with a blow to the chest.   Charlie swung and struck
Davie's raised forearm.   Neither wanted to fight.   They
were afraid of each other, and resentful against whatever
made this fight necessary.   Charlie was speaking as they
buffetted each other on the chest and arms.   The blows
were becoming pushes, both were blustering threateningly.
Their workmates crowded round, encouraging them,
pushing them together.   Suddenly Big Archie pushed
Davie.   Thrown off his balance, his short arm jab at
Charlie's chest, struck the other an agonising blow on
the throat.   With a grunt of pain Charlie swung his left
and struck Davie between the eyes, splitting the bridge
of his nose.   Blindly Davie groped for his friend,
caught the neck of his boiler suit, searching for his
throat.   They closed, reeled, and went down.   Big
Archie sent a sliver of tobacco juice on to the struggling
boys.   " Bate hell out av him, boy," he said with fine
impartiality.

THIS WE SHALL MAINTAIN

THE plump Strangford hills swelled up under their quilt of fields, and in their valleys littled fringed loughs like panes of gentle grey light, and a crumpled ribbon of road. Along the road travelled a boy in bright creaking boots and a Norfolk suit, the points of his tieless collar pulled together with a glittering brass pin. As he walked he murmured aloud passages from the metrical version of the Psalms, raising his eyes to the sky, and pausing only to gaze anxiously up the loanens leading from the road.

It being apparent from the silent loanens and the deserted road that he would have to travel alone, the boy quickened his pace, dividing his journey into stages ; frae Herron's gate tae Sarah's well, frae Sarah's well tae MucIlveen's, frae MucIlveen's tae the church-house.

> My strength is like a potsherd dried,
> My tongue it cleaveth fast
> Unto my jaws, and to the dust
> Of death thou brought me hast.

He wiped his streaming face with the lining of his cap, a veil of flies dancing after his perspiring head.

A tangle of boys and girls stood talking at the door of the church-house. One boy, in a heavy dark suit, the cuffs crusted with nose-drippings, his scalp shining through his clipped hair, darted from amongst them and grasped the newcomer by the arm. "Hi, Joe, Joe McGimpsey! Mester Cleland's started yer class. Gwan up noo, or ye'll no be let in." Joe pushed his way to the door and entered the church-house. He was pounced on by a bespectacled woman, his Sunday School teacher. "Ah, Joe, you're here at last. Come, sit on this form beside Aggie Gaw, and Mr. Cleland will take you in your turn."

At last Mr. Cleland raised his large discoloured hand and patted Aggie's curls as she rose with a smirk. Joe took her place and the other scholars slid their bottoms along the polished form. "Now, Joseph, whose class are you in?" asked Mr. Cleland with a wreathed smile.

"Miss Finlay's, Mester Cleland."

"An' have you come here this afternoon with all the lessons av the past year in your heart?"

"Yes," answered Joe, his hands crushed between his knees, his mind beating helplessly against the past.

"Well, tell me Joe, what is the chief end av Man?"

"Man's chief en'stooglorify God n'to'joy Him frever."

"*Very* good, Joe. An' what does it mean Joe, to enjoy Him for ever?"

Indignation, and a sense of panic welled up in the boy. Oul Cleland wus askin' him questions no in the buke. "It—it means that we shud be glad tae hae God fur ever."

"Good, Joe, good. But what do you mean by 'ever'?"

"It's when yer livin' an' after yer deid, when yer awa up in hivin'," answered Joe sullenly.

The questioning proceeded. Too often now, the

response was, I derno, Mester Cleland, and Mr. Cleland's demeanour became more querulous, more pained, more Joseph than Joe. The final catastrophic derno was spoken. Mr. Cleland, sucking the valence of his moustache in exasperation, raised his hand, the knuckles like chestnuts, and tapped Joe on the knee. "That'll do, Joe," he said. Joe arose and the next scholar took his place.

The scholars who lived in Raffrey parted from those who lived in Ballyhanna with a sod or two thrown between, or a bawled challenge to which distance lent impunity. The leader of the Raffrey group, amongst which was numbered Joe, was Tammas Miskimmin, the lad with the shaven head. When they had travelled a safe distance he effectively broke the tension and misgivings of the examinees around him by stabbing two fingers upwards at the distant church-house. "That's fur you, ma boul' Cleland!" he shouted, "I'm hung-ry yous yins," he continued, "who'll climb ower intae Darragh's fiel' an' hae a feed o' his kerrots?"

The children left the road and clambered into the carrot-field, over the gate and through gaps in the hedge, except Aggie Gaw, who continued her decorous way homeward. The sweet red roots were torn from the drills and their tails broken off on a rusty harrow. Suddenly a distant violent figure appeared on the skyline, and the children hurriedly regained the road, munching loudly, each attracting attention to himself by loud cries of appreciation.

As the last feathery head was tossed into the dyke Joe spied the crimson-olive shanks of Mrs. Conway's rhubarb. He pushed the iron gate ajar and, screened by red-currant bushes, snapped half-a-dozen leafed sticks at their ivory hooves and tossed them over the wall to his companions. In wry delight the children dragged out along the homeward road.

As they approached Gilmore's moss the smaller children instinctively herded together in collective safety against the weasels which infested the osiered sheughs, and which could, with ease, spring on a wean's chest and suck the life blood from his throat. Suddenly the loud clatter of Tammas's boots was heard on the road behind, and he came pounding up, rhubarb skin streaming from his mouth like crimson reins. " There's bags av whate in Gilmore's barn, come on an' hae a feed o' it ! " Several of the children turned queasy eyes on Tammas and put their hands to their stomachs. The only volunteer was Joe, so he and Tammas retraced their steps and turned off on to the little pad which ran to the barn, couched in nettles and ragweed. There they broke the curtain of chaff-hung web in the round glassless window and dropped down on to the polished black earth floor.

Tammas found a sampler and stabbed the sleek belly of a sack. The fat brown grain trickled down the sampler and then suddenly gushed over Tammas's palm as Joe sprang like a cock on to the bag. " Nae siller cups hid in this, Tam," he cried, thumping the sack and laughing down on the shorn ringwormed head of his friend. "Quit it, quit it, ye wee gett ye," cried Tammas springing up, " d'ye want oul' Gilmore findin' pickles av grain all ower his flure ? " He opened his young calloused hands and poured some of the wheat into Joe's palm. " Ate it up, Joe boy," he said.

They raised themselves up on a turnip-cutter and dropped out through the circular window. " Tammas," said Joe, stopping in the shade of a great beech, " dae ye think whun Abraham begat Zimran an' Jokshan an' Midian, did they ate rhubarb an' whate when they were wee weans, rinnin' aboot the land av Canaan ? " Tammas's dull brown eyes opened in bewilderment. " I derno, Joe," he said, " they maun well hae ate whate, but no' rhubarb. That wus brocht frae — Turkey, lang efter. But come on, wull ye, the ithers are all ower the Beech Hill."

Slowly Joe slipped down the muscular trunk of the beech until he was on his knees in the grass. " I'm no' goin', Tammas," he said, " I'm sick. Will ye put yer haun' tae ma heid till I throw aff ? " At last Joe raised his white face from the grass, wiping his chin with the heel of his hand. " Come on ye daft wee scitter, climb on ma back an' I'll carry ye," cried Tammas, " wull ye no' learn sense ? Maun ye always be gettin' yersel' sick or hurt ? " " The whate swells up inside av ye, Tammas," said Joe sleepily, his chin on Tammas's shoulder, his fair hair against Tammas's shaven head. Tammas lowered him at the head of McGimpsey's loanen. " Are ye fine, Joe ? " he asked. " I'm fine, Tammas," smiled Joe, swaying against the gatepost, " I'm goin' on hame."

Joe reached his bedroom before the second wave of sickness shook him. He tugged at the window, stiff with countless coats of white enamel, and vomited long and heavily. Then he lay with his head in the fragrant garden air, drowsily gazing down on a Gloire de Dijon, her golden head bowed under the weight of his sickness.

Four Sabbaths later Ballyhanna Meeting-house held a packed congregation. From the colourfulness of the pews, the sudden scuffles, the sharp rasp of heavy boots on the varnished wood and the chuckling roll of col-. lection pennies on the floor, it was evident that the youth of the townlands were there in full array, in soap-plastered hair, vivid head-ribbons and shapeless dub-bined boots. It was the Sabbath School Prize Day, and books in neat rows sat against the base of the pulpit and between the legs of the Communion table.

The Reverend Robert Watson descended the carpeted steps of his pulpit and approached the Communion rail. The Sabbath School Superintendent handed him two books for each successful scholar, one for Answering in Scripture, one for School Attendance. He flicked the covers open and read out the names inscribed on the ornate stickers. As he called, the scholars rose from the family pews and went down to the minister to receive their prizes. " Agnes Mary Gaw, First Prize for Attendance, First Prize for Answering in Scripture." Aggie strutted down the aisle, her short pigtail bobbing as she walked. " Joseph Neilly McGimpsey, First Prize for Attendance, Third Prize for Answering n Scripture." Joe dragged his legs along the stiff shins of his family whose eyes were fixed in an unwavering stare on the gilded characters on the font, God is Love. Only his aunt Lottie spoke. Her sibilant whisper followed him down the aisle, " *a Third Prize fur a McGimpsey*."

While leaving the meeting-house, Joe went out beside prize-flushed Aggie Gaw. Proudly she read the names of her prizes, " Wonders of the Seashore " for Attend-ance, " The Life of Mary Slessor " for Scripture

Answering. Joe opened his book and looked at the crude frontispiece of a warrior in armour and skins, Judas Maccabeus, Deliverer of Israel. " Luk at that, Aggie Gaw, a buke av giants. Ye're welcome tae yer cockleshells an' missionary weemin. Boy," he cried, " gie me a buke av fightin' men ! " Before Aggie could reply the voice of his aunt was heard : " Joe, come an' gie a haun' tae yoke the powny." The pony was harnessed and yoked and the family clambered into the trap. Not a word was spoken by the five people except for brief commands to the horse as he trotted along the levels or weaved his way up the hills.

The shame and affront on the McGimpseys was not one that could be removed by chastising Joe. The failure was moral rather than scholarly. It was a reflection on the family, a proof of their indifference to the Holy Word, a sign of their falling away in grace. That night Joe went early to his bed taking with him his prize. The wall at the foot of his bed was lined with shelves on which rested the prizes of decades of McGimpseys. Tired at last of reading, for like most third prizes it was an interesting book, he turned his lamp low, watched the death flickers of the wick on the low ceiling, and then fell asleep. He was awakened by his door being pushed open, and saw the white-gowned figure of his aunt in the doorway. By the light of the candle she carried, the boy saw her sunken cheeks and folded mouth, for she had removed her teeth. At last she spoke : " I thank the Good Man yer father's no' livin' tae see this day." The lip of the boy trembled, the flame of the withdrawn candle spread into a stratum of light in his swimming eyes. He turned his face to the face of Judas Maccabeus and wept.

DARK TENEMENT

By discreet enquiries amongst his more experienced friends Robert decided that in The Cupid he might find the answer to his question. The Cupid is a pub midway between Belfast's dockland and the City centre. It is a tiny, noisy and highly-coloured tavern where you pay a penny extra for your drinks, even draught. Its patrons are mostly sailors with shanty basses and gold rings in their ear, and occasional furtive business men. Beyond the door is an annexe, reserved according to the notice, for vocalists. Party songs, the notice proceeds, are discouraged, but here the singers are moved by nostalgia rather than politics, and the tavern trio, led by a skilled fiddle, move with more verve through *Sur le plancher des vaches*, than over *Dolly's Brae*.

To the right is the counter; to the left, behind a painted trellis hung with paper roses, is a shallow room around whose walls runs a mural of amorous devices drawn with more wit than draughtsmanship, lips, poets, winebottles and over the door marked LADIES, an obese cupid leers down the room, resting a wearied string arm. This shallow room is the tavern's heart, for here are the women, no pallid street-shadows, but rombustious queans stretching out their fat calves, and knocking back stout, egg-flip and other nutritious liquors.

Robert bought a glass of beer and carried it into the inner room. He sat down at a table at which three women and two men were drinking. The woman he sat beside, her bosom covered with a vast curved frontage of pink silk, slipped her arm inside his chair and plaited her fingers in his. " How's the body, dearie ? " she laughed, turning her bright beady eyes on him. " Never better " said Robert, " wha'll you have to drink ? " his eyes took in the others " wha'll you all have to drink ? " " Joe ! " cried the stout woman, " a little service, please ! " The barman came, selecting Robert instinctively with an upward nod of interrogation. " Same again all round " said Robert.

They raised their glasses to him, the women with smiles, the men with polite suspicion. Across the table, a young woman a shade slimmer and more than a shade prettier than her companions, eyed the drunken vivid face. As Pink Blouse opened an offensive with whispers and shiny red fingers the girl stood up, drawing her furs across her handsome shoulders, and passing round the table caught Robert's arm. " Come on, dearie," she said. " Take yer hands aff my friend, Rosie Poots ! " cried Pink Blouse reeling to her feet. The girl, with the heel of her hand, pushed her in the chest, and with a futile cry the stout woman slumped back into her chair. " Come away from that oul' targe " said the girl plucking Robert to his feet.

She led him out into the air, and still grasping his arm, piloted him towards the city. The sensation of taking this woman's arm, an endearment he had always hoarded for the girl he would love, vexed and thrilled Robert. It was as if a cell of his being had been broken into. She led him to a pub, quieter than the Cupid and Robert ordered drinks. " Are ye feelin' better, dearie ?"

asked Rosie. " Me ? I'm all right. What do we do now ? " " Well, it's gettin' late, an' I'm hungry." Robert drained his glass and stood up. " Let's go then " he said.

They had stew in a snack-house and then Rosie wanted coffee and hamburgers. Robert watched her as he sipped his coffee ; the neat shabby costume, the un-wrinkled stockings, the ludicrous grandeur of the dark fur tinged with silver. " Rosie " he said, " it seems funny to see you in a place like that " he jerked his thumb over his shoulder. She looked at him stonily. "You're about six drinks behind me, dearie " she said.

Because of the late Christmas shoppers they had to stand on the platform of the tram which took them out to Rosie's rooms. Now, to Robert's dismay the last gulped drinks were taking effect on his companion. By the time the tram was curving round Roarin' Hanna's statue she was singing at the top of her voice, her arms around Robert and the conductor. " Rosie, please ! Maybe somebody on this car knows me " whispered the young man desperately. In a second she had stopped Her fingers when she touched him were vibrant with sympathy. " Ach, dearie, you must be a lonely soul ! *Everybody* in this tram knows me ! They dismounted at the next stop, below a row of tall dark tenements.

" How about a drink ? " asked Rosie coaxingly as they crossed to the opposite pavement. " At this hour ? But it's long after closing time ! " Robert laughed. " I can fix that " she assured him, and turning the corner of the block, stopped at the darkened side door of a pub. She knocked rapidly three times, then twice slowly. In a few seconds the dragging of bolts was heard and the door opened sufficiently for a sibilant suspicious " Who's that ? " " It's Rosie, John. I've a friend here. Let us in, will ye ? " The door opened and the publican stared hard at Robert. " Come on in " he said at last, and they entered the darkened bar. " A bottle or a half 'un, dearie ? " asked Rosie. The young man scraped his nail around the milled edges of three coins in his pocket and felt the crisp note against his knuckles. " A bottle " he replied. The man reached down a tissued bottle, spinning it in his hands. " Six shillings " he said. Robert paid out the money and took the bottle under his arm. " Good night, John," said Rosie pecking at his cheek, " Merry Christmas," " Merry Christmas " said Robert. The man laughed and closed the door on their heels.

They rounded the face of the tenements, and Rosie stopping at a door, took a latchkey from her bag. " Here we are, dearie," she said pushing the door, which sucked and whispered as it opened. Robert groped towards the banisters, following the dim oscillation of her legs as they mounted flights of thin-carpeted stairs. She turned off down a lobby the walls of which glistened with moisture. Below a naked bulb burning at the end of the passage was a gas-stove, and a girl in a kimono industriously shaking a frying pan.

When they came closer Robert saw that she was crying. Rosie stopped to speak to her, then suddenly remembering Robert, turned and opened a door, and pushed him into the room beyond. He found himself in a large dishevelled apartment across the windows of which were drawn tawdry chintz curtains. A chinese vase at one end of the mantelpiece was paired at the

other by half a bottle of milk, and between them draped
an undergarment of frowsy lace and ribbons. In the
flickering hearth a teapot was embedded to its spout in
ashes and screwed cigarette packets. Drawing up a
bread bin with a disembowelled cushion on it, Robert
sat down before the fire.

The door opened and Rosie came in, pulling off her
fur. " Where's the bottle, dearie ? " she asked. " I
want to give Julie a drink. Dear help her, her man
didn't turn up, an' this Christmas Eve." She rummaged behind a screen and brought out a corkscrew and
a glass. " Men are rats, dearie " she said as she drew
the cork " some of them, anyway." She carried a
brimming glass out to the lobby.

When she returned, Robert had taken off his coat and
was unlacing his shoes, for his feet were sore. Until
now, Rosie had not touched upon the delicate subject of
her remuneration, lulled, no doubt, by Robert's liber-
ality on the question of drink, especially the bottle of
port. She now came to the point without preamble.
" It'll be a pound to stop here, dearie," she said. Robert
smiled tipsily and lifted his shoe, " ten shillings Rosie,"
he replied. " I said a quid " insisted Rosie, anger in
her voice. " O.K." said Robert with a gesture of dis-
missal, pulling his shoe on. " Oh, don't be so dam
quick," she said, rising to her feet. The clock on the
shelf pointed to midnight. Robert eased his shoe until
it was hanging from his toes, whilst Rosie stood over
him, plucking thoughtfully at her lip. " Fifteen
shillings, lovie," " Ten shillings, duckie," crowed
Robert. " Gor, but yer a mean wee squirt ! " she
cried, sweeping down the room. She came back to him,

" All right give me yer ten bob." Robert giggled weakly and dropped his shoe.

At about four in the morning he awoke with a parched mouth and holding the segments of his head together, made his way into the lobby. At the stove, with her back to him, was the girl in the kimono. She faced him as he closed the door softly and he saw that her face was damp with tears. " Still crying ? " he asked, touching her shoulder, " Wait, I'll be back in a minute." He reeled down the lobby, fending himself off from the walls. When he came back she was gone, but at the noise of the boards creaking under his feet she put her head round the door and signed him to come in. When he entered she looked expectantly at his hands. " You wouldn't have a drink on you, would you ? " she asked. Robert smiled and nodded " I'll get you one " he said.

" Call me Julie " said the girl, as Robert put the port bottle down, " what's your name ? " " Tommie " he answered, " have you a glass ? " She set two glasses beside the bottle, and Robert lifting one, splashed it half full of the dull red liquid. As she drank it, he looked around the room. . . . An armchair pulled close to the now darkened window, the tumbled bed with both pillows dented, the nervous eating and drinking, all spoke of a restless lonely woman.

Julie set her glass down, reading his thoughts. " Did Miss Poots tell you ? " she asked. " Yes, she said something about your friend not turning up." " Was that all ? " " Yes " answered Robert " that was all." She put one arm around his shoulders and ran her hand over his face and hair. " You're a nice boy " she said.

Some time after, as Robert poured out fresh drinks,

he said to her, " Are you still sorry he didn't turn up ? "
" No, I'm not." She turned her face to him. " I'll
tell you something queer. He never took his trousers
off. Even from the beginning," she continued thoughtfully, " I felt he didn't love me." Robert, balancing
a glass of port on his navel, leaned back to consider this
novel attitude to Love. He raised himself to look down
on her dim face. " Do you really believe that's love ?
Is that what it means to you ? " Without warning
Julie flung herself around and struck the astounded
youth in the face, the ring on her wedding finger cutting
his cheek. " You beast ! " she shouted, " You ignorant
young cur ! Get out, get out will you ! " She crouched
on the bed, her teeth chattering with rage. " How dare
you " she muttered over and over, " God, how dare
you " Robert stood with his palms pressed to the
wall. " I beg your pardon " he whispered into the
darkness.

As he spoke, there was a movement in the chair by the
window and a head rose slowly over the back, peering
into the room. In the dim morning light Robert's
gaping eyes made out the head of a very old woman, her
thrawn neck protruding from a flannel nightgown. She
was staring at the woman on the bed. Suddenly she
looked at Robert, her tongue flickering over her pale
lips. " Leave the bottle, son," she whispered. With a
cry he gathered up his shirt and fled. As he crossed the
lobby, he heard the mutter of bells from the city.

After he had dressed, he stood looking down at Rosie.
She lay in a stupor, snoring heavily. A strand of her
hair straggled across the pillow and he leaned forward to
touch it gently. It means more than that, even to you,

he thought. He was elevated and drunk as he went down through the deserted house. The street door sighed and whistled behind him.

From the church across the way the early Christmas worshippers were departing, sleek backs, dapper shoes, woolly pleated children, whilst in the dim church the choir raised their voices in a triumphant carol. He crossed over and grasping the railings, peered inside. The light poured down through the glassy draperies of a saint high in the painted wall. The organist mustered his choir for the final pean. Robert gazed up at the lucent figure. You've been at it for two thousand years, he said, tell me, have you found the answer ? *Gloria*, they shouted exultantly, *Gloria in excelsis Deo* !

OLD CLAY NEW EARTH

THE mourners radiated out from the cottage parlour where the coffin lay, to the edge of the sunless close. There, in the parlour, the minister with the husband and sons knelt in the intimacy of prayer. I, who had loved her and been loved in turn could have been there, but I sat in the kitchen with the women. I heard the minister come up through the labryinth of little rooms and go out into the close. The eldest son followed to beckon to the undertaker; all was ready; now they might bolt the lid down on the ivory face and slender hands. The coffin was carried out of the gloom into the light. The neighbours who had stood under the rowan trees, slapping their legs with twigs and talking in undertones of crops and cattle, took off their hats and shuffled into awkward file.

They offered me a place at the carrying of the coffin down to the loanen. This, they thought, was a privilege. For my part, I was preoccupied in avoiding the heels of the man in front. Furthermore, the man on the other side was taller than I, and the heavy wood bit into my shoulder.

The hearse has been driven down the narrow loanen to the farm gates where we now stooped to slide the coffin on to the rollers. The undertaker moved with authority amongst us. Custom has made it in him a property of easiness, and custom had lent him a sombreness which repelled me. He spoke with deference to the sons, showed no impatience with the roller locks, laid his whip gently on the horses' flanks. Where does his sympathy knit between the anguish of the youngest son and the ruddy young farmer from a distant place across the lough who now jokes in whispers at the tail of the cortege ?

I had often heard old men speak of her loveliness. I had only known her when she was old, but the coiling hair, now white, the finely pencilled nose, the rounded chin, these were remnants of that beauty when she had been a fair-haired creature, and these bent and bearded, men her lovers. She had been an imperious woman, but gracious when stratagems demanded it. She had whipped me, which women with a greater right had never done. Sometimes unjustly, as when she accused me of tormenting with sticks the pike in the sweet well at the bottom of our garden. Sometimes by instinct, when she saw a fowl limp across the close. But when I entered a forbidden field and was trampled by a young bullock, or fell off a new tarred roof, she would take me home without reproach, butter my bruises and comfort me with tea and sugared potato bread.

They buried her in a graveyard overlooking Strangford. The grave and the graves on either side were filled with the dead of our people, some of the stones sunken and defaced, some gone. From below the high walls of the graveyard, the fields ran down like a russet shawl to the slaty waters of the lough. To-day the autumn winds were weaving their nuances of blue and grey across the stretches and among the many islands. The sycamore, stooping over the wall, held the wind and spattered us with drops, as the coffin was lowered by groaning hempen ropes and its futile silken cords.

At the head of the grave, his polished boots sunk in the red earth, the young minister read the verses of comfort. Now only the dead woman's relatives stood at the graveside, the neighbours withdrawn in clusters, whispering or scraping with their sticks the moss from old lettering. *Or ever the silver cord be loosed, or the golden bowl be broken, or the pitcher be broken at the fountain, or the wheel broken at the cistern* . . . . .

She had been a woman who had felt deeply and mourned little. A peasant, she had lived as the women who worked with their hands, to accept contentment and relinquish ecstacy ; to bear children, to listen to sorrows, and be filled with wisdom. She had lived in the God of her forefathers and believed in the life eternal. She had lived her faith to her children and *they* had believed. Now I saw their dark sad clothes and the misery of their faces. What did they mourn and what was lost to them ? The essence of her being, or the broken vase now laid in the earth ? How human that those who believe in immortality should mourn.

As the preacher drew back there was a sudden dislodgement of the soil, and a round clay-filled thing hampered by muddy streamers trundled to my feet. I heard the man behind me catch his breath and glimpsed his aged distorted face thrust over my shoulder. " It's Tammie's first yin " he breathed, " I wud ha' kenned her by her lang black hair ! " I looked up to where Tom stood ; he was gazing over the lough, following the flight of three swans as they toiled across the sky. With a twist of the blade the digger spun the skull back into the earth.

Now came the time to cover in the grave. A look passed between the eldest son and the father, and the father picking up a clod handed it to the youngest son. The lad stepped forward to the grave's edge and crumbled the soil down on the dead. The diggers hitched at their belts and bounded great slices of clay into the grave, straining and grunting, pushing with their knees against the shovel shafts.

From the corners of the graveyard the mourners drifted towards the raw grave, pressing hands, whispering sympathy. Some went out to the carriages to bring in the stiff smiling wreaths, shouting with unnecessary force at the horses to stand still. As the last mourner came through the gates, and the last carriage door was slammed, I felt the sycamore throw up its head and push its roots towards this new earth.

THE MOURNE PRESS
Newcastle, Co. Down